The Executioner loomed over the dying enemy gunner

"Kuschka's gone on to Lebanon, hasn't he?"

"American, you will never catch him or defeat all of us." Defiance hardened the Russian's face. "An entire army is in the Bekaa Valley. Another army is waiting in Karachi...."

Bolan stared into the strange laughing look in the hardman's eyes.

"Go get yourselves killed. I just told you where to find them. I send you to die by Kuschka's hand."

The Russian sighed deeply, then his head lolled to one side.

Lebanon. Pakistan. Kuschka had a full plate of pickups and deliveries. Well, Bolan intended to be on hand to make certain the surviving enemy hordes choked on their own blood.

MACK BOLAN ®
The Executioner

#167 Double Action
#168 Blood Price
#169 White Heat
#170 Baja Blitz
#171 Deadly Force
#172 Fast Strike
#173 Capitol Hit
#174 Battle Plan
#175 Battle Ground
#176 Ransom Run
#177 Evil Code
#178 Black Hand
#179 War Hammer
#180 Force Down
#181 Shifting Target
#182 Lethal Agent
#183 Clean Sweep
#184 Death Warrant
#185 Sudden Fury
#186 Fire Burst
#187 Cleansing Flame
#188 War Paint
#189 Wellfire
#190 Killing Range
#191 Extreme Force
#192 Maximum Impact
#193 Hostile Action
#194 Deadly Contest
#195 Select Fire
#196 Triburst
#197 Armed Force
#198 Shoot Down
#199 Rogue Agent
#200 Crisis Point
#201 Prime Target
#202 Combat Zone
#203 Hard Contact
#204 Rescue Run

#205 Hell Road
#206 Hunting Cry
#207 Freedom Strike
#208 Death Whisper
#209 Asian Crucible
#210 Fire Lash
#211 Steel Claws
#212 Ride the Beast
#213 Blood Harvest
#214 Fission Fury
#215 Fire Hammer
#216 Death Force
#217 Fight or Die
#218 End Game
#219 Terror Intent
#220 Tiger Stalk
#221 Blood and Fire
#222 Patriot Gambit
#223 Hour of Conflict
#224 Call to Arms
#225 Body Armor
#226 Red Horse
#227 Blood Circle
#228 Terminal Option
#229 Zero Tolerance
#230 Deep Attack
#231 Slaughter Squad
#232 Jackal Hunt
#233 Tough Justice
#234 Target Command
#235 Plague Wind
#236 Vengeance Rising
#237 Hellfire Trigger
#238 Crimson Tide
#239 Hostile Proximity
#240 Devil's Guard
#241 Evil Reborn
#242 Doomsday Conspiracy

DON PENDLETON'S
THE EXECUTIONER®
DOOMSDAY CONSPIRACY

A GOLD EAGLE BOOK FROM
WORLDWIDE®

TORONTO • NEW YORK • LONDON
AMSTERDAM • PARIS • SYDNEY • HAMBURG
STOCKHOLM • ATHENS • TOKYO • MILAN
MADRID • WARSAW • BUDAPEST • AUCKLAND

First edition February 1999
ISBN 0-373-64242-3

Special thanks and acknowledgment to
Dan Schmidt for his contribution to this work.

DOOMSDAY CONSPIRACY

Printed in U.S.A.

Power in defense of freedom is greater than power
in behalf of tyranny and oppression.

—Malcolm X
1925-1965

Power, like a desolating pestilence,
Pollutes whate'er it touches…

—Percy Bysshe Shelley
Queen Mab (1813), III

The temptation of unlimited power proves too much for
many, corrupting morals, provoking unconscionable
behavior. We must all be accountable for our actions.

—Mack Bolan

THE
MACK BOLAN®
LEGEND

Nothing less than a war could have fashioned the destiny of the man called Mack Bolan. Bolan earned the Executioner title in the jungle hell of Vietnam.

But this soldier also wore another name—Sergeant Mercy. He was so tagged because of the compassion he showed to wounded comrades-in-arms and Vietnamese civilians.

Mack Bolan's second tour of duty ended prematurely when he was given emergency leave to return home and bury his family, victims of the Mob. Then he declared a one-man war against the Mafia.

He confronted the Families head-on from coast to coast, and soon a hope of victory began to appear. But Bolan had broken society's every rule. That same society started gunning for this elusive warrior—to no avail.

So Bolan was offered amnesty to work within the system against terrorism. This time, as an employee of Uncle Sam, Bolan became Colonel John Phoenix. With a command center at Stony Man Farm in Virginia, he and his new allies—Able Team and Phoenix Force—waged relentless war on a new adversary: the KGB.

But when his one true love, April Rose, died at the hands of the Soviet terror machine, Bolan severed all ties with Establishment authority.

Now, after a lengthy lone-wolf struggle and much soul-searching, the Executioner has agreed to enter an "arm's-length" alliance with his government once more, reserving the right to pursue personal missions in his Everlasting War.

Marseilles, France

The night was about to turn ugly with sudden death.

Five thugs entered the waterfront bar—three filed through the fishnet-draped front door, while two more slowly walked in from the narrow hallway that led to the back alley. Bulges made by holstered weapons were visible beneath their coats. Mack Bolan's first impression was that they looked like seasoned killers, eyes cold and reptilian, with the lifeless gaze of men who shed blood for either money or pleasure—or both.

The soldier already suspected the meet would go south in gunplay, and long before the ominous message he had delivered by phone to Pinchot Import and Export. It was simply a question of who would get in the first killing shot.

As a group they looked Bolan's way, sizing the lone man in black. He was sitting at a large wooden round table, his back to the wall. A large mug of beer was at his fingertips, exactly as he had informed Pinchot. Bolan had called the meet, using himself as bait, but they had chosen the place. Naturally the Executioner knew he was walking into a trap on enemy turf, but he carried ample firepower, and he had backup. The hardforce, he believed, worked—perhaps unwittingly—for an organization comprised of former U.S. military men and intelligence agents. So far, Bolan had very few clues as to what the organization was, much less its agenda. He was searching for answers, and a lead to resume the hunt for his enemies any way he could find them.

The lead hardman, shoulder-length white hair spilling from his black watch cap, nodded at his two companions across the bar. From there the two thugs headed for the crowd at the bar to obviously cover the rear. White Hair and his comrades began to snake through the scattered tables, the clouds of smoke and patrons of Latin, Arab and African descent.

Bolan surveyed his surroundings. Other than its seedy ambience and the obvious prostitution, the bar could have been one of a thousand on any waterfront in the world. Long bar, plenty of liquor shelves, tables, stools, one harpoon, fishnets and anchors on the walls. With back rooms and a second story where painted ladies took their johns.

The soldier wasn't about to trust first impressions. The patrons appeared to be a rough-and-tumble crowd of sailors, soldiers, prostitutes, perhaps even narcotics traffickers, pimps. In general everyone was drinking, smoking and grab-assing for a night of fun and games or nailing down some illicit deal. But this was Marseilles, after all, and organized crime was the seamy underbelly of France's number-three city and largest port. Scores of ships from east and west docked in Marseilles, many loaded with contraband, chiefly narcotics.

It was a load of cocaine, valued at somewhere in the neighborhood of one billion dollars after cutting for street sale, but now sunk to the bottom of the Caribbean, that had led Bolan to this moment. He knew the loss inflicted on the enemy wouldn't go unavenged. There was a good chance the hardforce had come to shoot first, and last. End of discussion.

Less than six hours earlier the Executioner, along with Jack Grimaldi, Stony Man Farm's ace pilot, had landed on a military flight on a secured private airstrip north of the city. Thanks to Hal Brognola, arrangements for the two men to operate in France—helped by nervous authorities at the U.S. Embassy in Paris—had been made. Blacksuits from Stony Man Farm had secured a base in the Pyrenees from which the two Americans could operate and move in on their principal targets—in time, though, and when the Executioner had gauged the strength and numbers of his quarry.

First Bolan needed to lay the groundwork for rooting out the players in a shadowy international conspiracy. The Farm had put together an impressive shopping list for Bolan detailing potential coconspirators on the European continent.

Unfortunately the big game had managed to escape Bolan.

But if the traitorous ex–Special Forces Major Ben Calhoun and William McBain, "retired" five-star general, had come to Marseilles with their mercenary army, then Bolan and Grimaldi could end the enemy's reign of terrorism that had begun in New York, blazed a path for the two men through South Florida, only to elude them in Colombia.

Bolan lifted the beer to his lips, then muttered into the minimike beneath the lapel of his long overcoat, "Show time."

With no earpiece he knew he couldn't alert his visitors they were audio-monitored. Grimaldi was waiting in their rental sedan in an alley across from the bar. If he heard the phrase "This is not good," he knew to come running and hit the hardmen from their blind side with his Uzi submachine gun on full-auto. Of course, logic dictated the thugs had their own cover outside, perhaps even upstairs or already planted in the crowd. But Bolan was gambling they were right then showing their entire force, unthreatened by a single American.

As the trio settled into chairs facing him, Bolan felt the weight of the Beretta 93-R in its shoulder holster and the .44 Magnum Desert Eagle riding on his hip. Spare clips for both weapons were in the pockets of his coat. Whether they were crazy enough to just open fire in a public place remained to be seen. Even still, the soldier was ready to draw both weapons in an eye blink and send it all to hell. Pinchot was hiding, but Bolan was about to change that.

"You don't look like René Pinchot," Bolan said to White Hair, as he recalled the intel photo of the Marseilles shipping magnate that had been faxed from Stony Man Farm earlier.

"My name is Brousseau," White Hair said, his voice thickly accented. "Monsieur Pinchot is anxious to speak personally with the individual who claims to have destroyed a vessel belonging to him and his associates. If what you claim is true, you have greatly upset people who do not like to be upset."

"I'll bring some tissues so they can dry their eyes."

Brousseau scowled. "And your name is...?"

"Monsieur Problem."

The gray eyes flickered over Bolan's face, then White Hair chuckled and glanced at the men on either side. "Indeed. So, you are the one who claims to have sunk a legitimate seafaring vessel of ours from Cartagena."

Bolan's lips tightened in a grim smile. "A dozen men opened fire on me from the deck with automatic weapons. Maldonado is dead. I killed him myself. So your Cali connection, and the people you work for, has been permanently severed. There was a load of cocaine on the ship that belonged, on paper, to Max Tielig of Munich. Pinchot is Tielig's boy here in Marseilles, which is the gateway for most heroin flowing to the United States and for cocaine coming into Europe. The ship's crew was checked out, and all of them had known criminal records or mercenary backgrounds. An F-15E unloaded twelve tons of bombs and missiles on your 'legitimate seafaring vessel.' I'm satisfied there wasn't a single man on board who didn't know what they were hauling. That's history. What I want now is Pinchot's cooperation in helping me to contact the men who purchased that load of dope.''

Brousseau studied Bolan for a long moment, his massive jaw clenching. ''And just what is it you are offering in return for Monsieur Pinchot's cooperation?''

''A little longer life.''

Brousseau and his companions chuckled. ''And I am sure you have brought others with you to Marseilles to cause us grief in the event you do not get this cooperation.''

Bolan injected ice into his look and tone. ''What I've brought is a bad attitude and the determination to track down the men I'm looking for. Now, do we carry on a song and dance in this dump, or do you take me to Mr. Pinchot?''

''But, of course, we will go see the man now.''

''We'll take my vehicle. You'll come with me.''

''No, no. He is not at his warehouse. He is close. Within walking distance.''

Bolan's instincts flared to life. They wanted to get him outside, isolated, then make their move. Or did they? Upstairs he glimpsed a large figure trolling the landing, looking down his way. A large bulge was visible beneath the guy's suit coat. It was meant to go down right there.

"You can even keep your weapons," Brousseau said, glancing at Bolan's coat. "A show of good faith. We will walk out of here together. You can even stick your weapon in my ribs. Would you agree, however, to having two of my men in back of us?"

It was too easy, and too treacherous at the same time. A walking phalanx, marching a lone American to his death.

"Listen, my American friend," Brousseau said, "if we want you dead, you are dead. This is Marseilles. People get killed here all the time, and the police, they are both corrupt and incompetent. You have no reason to believe we mean to do anything other than take you to Monsieur Pinchot so you may get your information."

"You're saying I could just disappear and no one would be the wiser, much less care."

Brousseau shrugged. "It is not our wish."

"Let's take a walk," the Executioner agreed.

They rose together. There was something in Brousseau's look the soldier suddenly trusted less than ever.

Bolan was moving around the table when he spotted the switchblade flicking open and arcing for his throat.

2

Expecting gunmetal instead of razor-sharp steel, Bolan was already drawing the .44 Magnum Desert Eagle. Obviously the thugs had hoped for a quick and quiet kill. One slash across the throat of the lone American, fading into the crowd while he collapsed, choking on his own blood.

Years of surviving countless do-or-die situations had honed Bolan's reflexes and instincts to react with all the sudden explosiveness of a detonating hand grenade. Besides, the thug had already tipped his hand by digging into his coat pocket, savage aggression lighting his eyes.

Bolan darted back, felt the slipstream of the blade sweeping past his flesh. Cold rage seized him. The thug had thrown everything he had behind the attack, even baring crooked teeth in a snarl or a half smile. The expression vanished, and the thug stumbled into the muzzle of the Executioner's hand cannon. A thick wooden pole stood directly behind the knifeman. Aware of the .44 slug's muzzle velocity and the crowd of unsuspecting patrons who might take the exiting bullet, Bolan squeezed the trigger and blew the guy's guts out his back. The impact lifted the hardman off his feet, hurtled him backward. Both man and bullet were absorbed by the pole.

One of the dead man's comrades stood, frozen,

watching the body crumple into a boneless sprawl as if in disbelief the attack failed. He became the Executioner's number-two target.

A moment of shocked silence descended, then pandemonium erupted. People scattered as the hardmen at the bar hauled out Skorpion machine pistols. Bolan glimpsed a compact subgun leaping into the hands of the watcher upstairs.

Screams and bellowed curses rent the air. Women ran or dropped to the floor while men nose-dived for cover or bolted for exits. With patrons racing in all directions, creating a human stampede, it was difficult at first for either Bolan or his enemies to get a clear line of fire.

Still, no sooner had he shot the first thug than the Executioner swung his aim and blew the hardman on his left off his feet just as the guy was pulling a large-caliber handgun.

For some reason Brousseau was already retreating, clawing for a weapon inside his coat. He grabbed a woman as a shield against Bolan's gun, before his legs clipped a chair. Brousseau and the woman tumbled to the floor in a tangle of arms and legs.

Crouching, Bolan fired the Desert Eagle on the run as bullets stitched the wall above his head, raking the pole. Downrange the soldier ventilated the chest of a Skorpion gunner, sending the hardman flipping over the bar, his Czech machine pistol chattering out rounds at the ceiling. Catching sight of a massive pump shotgun wielded in the hands of the bartender, Bolan suspected his troubles had only just begun. Grimaldi was on the way, no doubt, but the police could seal off the place any second. Detainment by the local law was an unacceptable fate for the soldier.

If it even got to that point.

A mirror shattered into countless fragments in Bolan's wake. He rolled over a fishnet-covered railing and dropped on a landing halfway up the stairs. The subgun chattered above him, and a head poked over the railing. The watcher tried to track Bolan with long bursts of autofire that whined off iron and splintered wood.

The bartender and the lone Skorpion gunman cut loose at the same instant, the roar of their weapons drowning the screaming and crashing of tables and chairs.

Bolan crouched behind the railing, then popped up and nailed the bartender, throwing him back into the liquor shelves under the impact of the .44 slug. A minefield of glass blew around the bar as the huge figure toppled from sight with shotgun.

The attack signaled Bolan two critical items. One, the owner was part of the ambush. Second, and worst of all, the enemy who had eluded Bolan and Grimaldi from across the Atlantic had identified them, alerted their French counterparts to their potential arrival and obviously sent a killing crew on a search-and-destroy.

The Executioner ducked behind the rail as wood exploded from a barrage of gunfire. He saw the upstairs gunner lean over the railing, firing for all he was worth. A line of slugs raked the rail where Bolan was a moment ago. The Executioner seized a moment to draw a bead on his upstairs problem. A squeeze of the big gun, and a .44 Magnum slug drilled through the soft flesh below the gunman's jaw, all but blowing off the top of his head.

It was then Bolan saw the Skorpion gunman grab a woman. She flailed in the enemy's grasp as he staggered for Bolan, holding back on the machine pistol's trigger.

JACK GRIMALDI came in shooting. Both of his targets were cradling mini-Uzis, cocking bolts, shoving aside men and women as the duo headed for the bedlam beyond the back hallway. Holding back on the trigger of his Uzi submachine gun, Grimaldi stitched the two-man team up their spines, all the way to the backs of their heads on a rising line of 9 mm Parabellum manglers. Gritted teeth and bulging eyes spun toward the ace pilot before the red ruins of the duo toppled into the barroom.

Grimaldi surged on, checking each doorway and his rear for any sign of hidden shooters. Other than women in various states of undress and recoiling inside their rooms at the sight of the lean man in the black topcoat brandishing the SMG, no one moved on the Stony Man pilot.

Only moments ago Grimaldi had seen the reinforcements disgorge from a Lexus to join their five comrades from the Mercedes-Benz. Grimaldi had listened to the exchange between Bolan and Brousseau, not liking the Frenchman's tone. Feeling the meet would blow in violence, Grimaldi waited in the alley until the first of several familiar retorts of the Executioner's .44 Magnum Desert Eagle boomed over his radio earpiece, sending Grimaldi racing for the back door.

Even before the meet, Grimaldi didn't like the idea of the big guy baiting the opposition and dropping himself into an ambush. But Bolan had explained it was only logical the recipients of the drug shipment would be alerted about the disaster that had dropped on them from the sky, thanks to Grimaldi's F-15E strike. The enemy would possibly be waiting for its hunters in Marseilles, holed up, regrouping. The idea was to get the enemy out of the shadows, running for them, hell-bent on shedding their blood.

Obviously Bolan's angle of attack had worked.

Ahead the human herd was thinning out. People were still scurrying everywhere, barreling into one another, falling to the floor, rising to run again. Grimaldi took one look at the wild-eyed gunman with the barking machine pistol and female shield, and knew Bolan was in danger of getting pinned down.

For a heartbeat the advancing Skorpion gunner was distracted by the sight of his comrades pitching from the hall. It was long enough for the woman to show a brazen display of fighting spirit. She threw an elbow into the gunman's nose, drawing a spray of blood and a yelp from the guy. She broke free of his grasp, but the gunman, either in a blind rage or panic, triggered a short burst of slugs into her back. As she screamed and fell to the floor, Grimaldi opened fire with his SMG. The gunner took the force of the slugs full in the chest, and the Stony Man pilot heard the thunder of the .44 Desert Eagle a second later. The gunman was dead in the air as he was hurled backward to land on a table, crushing it to matchsticks.

A giant figure with white hair loomed from somewhere in the middle of the barroom, a large revolver in his hand. Grimaldi didn't waste a second. He squeezed off a burst just as the Desert Eagle roared again to send the white-haired giant on an airborne course. Shredded by the warriors' streams of lead, he thudded on the landing near the front door.

Grimaldi made eye contact with Bolan as he rounded the corner, then caught sight of something else—a small man with slicked-back hair, dressed in a fancy silk suit, was barging from a doorway behind the bar. He gripped a pistol, and he seemed prepared to start shooting. Then the guy made a judgment call that saved his life. He dropped his pistol and raised his hands.

Grimaldi trained his Uzi on the guy as Bolan asked, "You own this dump?"

With a shaky nod the guy answered, "*Oui*, I mean, yes. I am Sarpries."

"I take it you want to talk to him?" Grimaldi asked.

Bolan checked their surroundings. At the moment it was only the three of them breathing in the slaughterhouse. "And maybe then some. Grab him. We're out of here."

Grimaldi made a beeline for the owner. Quick and rough, he frisked Sarpries, came up with a switchblade from a coat pocket. One glance at the carnage as he followed Bolan out of there, and the ace pilot knew things were just heating up in Marseilles. The night was still very young.

3

North of Vieux Port a nervous and agitated Sarpries guided the two men toward Pinchot Import and Export. Bolan had ridden in the back seat with their prisoner while Grimaldi drove them through the crowded streets in tight silence. So far, no threat, legal or otherwise, had shown up on their tail.

Bolan gave the grim industrial docks and warehouses ahead a hard surveillance. The yachts, fishing boats and other pleasure craft now yielded to the big container ships, moored to the massive docks.

"Find a place and park," Bolan told Grimaldi.

"You're going to get us past the front gate, Sarpries," the soldier continued. "No fuss, no muss on the way for a visit with Pinchot. If we do have an unexpected surprise waiting for us, your career as a pimp ends tonight. I'm sure he's waiting to hear from the crew he sent. You know where his office is?"

"In the main warehouse."

"So, you've been there. How many gunmen does he keep on hand?"

"It depends."

"Well, let's call this a special occasion. Ballpark figure."

"Could be as many as ten. Of course, you managed to kill his best."

"Give my friend directions to the front gate."

Scowling, Sarpries told Grimaldi to keep driving down the narrow street. Dark buildings rose on either side of the sedan. There were lights on in a few windows around them, with an occasional shadow moving down a bisecting alley. But all appeared eerily still and silent. Even the docks and ships were ominously devoid of any activity. It struck Bolan as no mere coincidence the shipyard had the appearance of being shut down. They were expected, if the hit at the bar failed.

Ahead Bolan saw the Pinchot sign over the massive front gate leading to the shipyard. Strangely the front gate looked slightly ajar. There was a guard booth, but the soldier didn't see any sign of security out front. Something felt wrong.

"What is it you wish me to do?" Sarpries asked as Grimaldi parked between two buildings in a tight alley, then killed the engine.

"Obviously you have some idea who we are," Bolan said.

"Indeed, bad news travels fast. If you two are who I think you are, then your minutes here in Marseilles are numbered."

"It would seem we're worth more dead than alive, all right. Do you know of any Americans who have come to visit Pinchot?"

"I do not follow Pinchot around all day, asking questions and spying on him."

"You're a pimp, a man with his fingers in a lot of pies. You helped your pal Pinchot set us up. You survive by knowing what goes on around you, in the street and beyond. I suspect you didn't land your bar through charm and good looks, which means you're connected to organized crime here in the city. You know more

than you want me to think you do.'' Bolan pulled the
Desert Eagle and jammed the muzzle in the Frenchman's ribs. ''Talk to me. The truth can be very
liberating.''

Sarpries grunted, and his eyes widened in fear. ''Very
well. I understand some Americans were here today but
they are gone—where I do not know. I hear other for-
eigners have paid Pinchot a visit. Russians, I hear. Then
some Colombians apparently dropped by on Pinchot
earlier this evening.''

Bolan hid his surprise, saw Grimaldi look at him in
the rearview. ''You're saying the drug shipment from
Cartagena, sailing under the supposed 'legitimate' front
of Max Tielig, was going to the Russian Mafia?''

''It would appear so—that is, until rumor spread that
it was sunk by a fighter jet in the Caribbean. I strongly
suspect you two know something about that, am I correct? Whatever. If you caused them to lose their shipment, that is why the Russians, the Americans and the
Colombians have been to see Pinchot. Marseilles is
crawling with foreign killers.''

''To field an ambush.''

''How astute you are. They know you are here. When
Pinchot called to inform me of all his uninvited visitors,
he was angry and worried.''

''You two are pretty tight.''

''Whatever, his men often frequent my establishment.
I give them services—Pinchot offers protection. Anyway, I was told there would be trouble in my place
when a certain big American with cold eyes would
show up in my place of business dressed in black. It
would seem many dangerous people are interested in
you two, and what happened at my place is only the

beginning. Surely they have backup plans to kill you two.''

"Pinchot, I assume, offered money to you to look the other way when I was supposed to take a quick slash across the throat.''

Sarpries hesitated, then nodded. "You intend to kill me because of that?''

"No," Bolan said. "You're simply going to get us in to see Pinchot. Tell me, is there usually a guard at the front gate?''

"Around the clock.''

"You know what I'm thinking?'' Grimaldi said to Bolan.

"More trouble," Bolan answered.

"Sarpries," he went on, "listen carefully to me. Whether you live or die in the next few minutes is up to you. You're to stay beside me at all times. If there's another trap set by Pinchot, you'll die first. If you live, it doesn't matter to us who you run to and sound the alarm. Pinchot has been fingered as a major importer of narcotics, and is suspected of running a slavery ring that brings women from the Far East to Marseilles," Bolan said, recalling the Intel Stony Man Farm had gathered on the underworld in Marseilles. "He does his business directly with your French don here in the city, Pierre Carreaux.''

Sarpries chuckled nervously. "So you know things which are common knowledge. You think you can dismantle the Marseilles underworld here, just two men? You are fools. There are Colombians and Russians here in Marseilles, and they are connected to the shipment I believe you two destroyed. Whatever business happens in this city, Pierre Carreaux not only knows about but demands a certain percentage.''

"I'll visit the boss of bosses in time. Get out, Sarpries."

Grimaldi was already out the door, moving and opening the trunk as Bolan exited the vehicle after Sarpries. The two soldiers shed their coats, opting for speed and accessibility to hardware. Quickly, while keeping one eye on their surroundings, they took what they needed from the trunk. Bolan fitted a mini-Uzi in a special shoulder holster opposite the Beretta, took spare clips for the piece, two frag grenades and attached everything to his combat webbing. Grimaldi slipped a holstered Llama .45ACP autopistol around his shoulder, the magazine housing Winchester 230-grain rounds for maximum stopping power. Likewise, spare clips for the Uzi subgun and backup piece were fixed to his webbing.

Bolan unleathered the Beretta 93-R and attached its sound suppressor. He grabbed Sarpries by the arm, shoving him ahead. The soldier already suspected they were walking into another trap, but there was no other way than to hit the enemy head-on. The list of enemy numbers was multiplying with each new phase of the mission. With luck a body count would lead to the main targets.

If nothing else, Stony Man Farm had pinpointed the château in the Pyrenees that belonged to McBain. Bolan's goal was simple enough on the surface: flush out whatever enemies were in Marseilles, seething over the loss of their dope. Shave the numbers, hit the enemy wherever they could. Mop up, move on and eliminate Calhoun, McBain and whoever else was part of the conspiracy with its mystery agenda.

Easier said, Bolan knew, than done.

Light shone from domed overheads to guide Bolan and Grimaldi to the front gate. Beyond the gate,

18-wheelers, forklifts, garbage bins and a few parked vehicles were scattered around the loading bays. It was at the guard booth that Bolan found there might be more players involved here besides Pinchot.

Sarpries gasped at the sight of the guard sprawled over his chair. One look, and Bolan saw the neat red hole between the guard's eyes.

Bolan and Grimaldi exchanged grim looks, then the soldier ushered Sarpries past the front gate. The pimp was leading them toward the loading bay of the large warehouse when the Executioner heard the muffled retort of weapons fire from inside the building.

Angling for the structure, Bolan turned to check the rear when two shadows popped through the front gate. The shadows were armed with assault rifles, swinging the muzzles up to draw target acquisition.

At the same instant Bolan shouted a warning to Grimaldi, Sarpries wrenched free of the soldier's grasp and the shadow gunmen cut loose with their assault rifles.

Panic cost Sarpries his life, but the Frenchman's flight across Bolan's path may have saved the Executioner.

Even still, as soon as the opening retorts of AK-47 autofire hit the air, Bolan was already diving away from the tracking bullets. Crying out in pain, Sarpries absorbed the initial 7.62 mm barrage. The Frenchman was spun by the storm of lead and sent skidding to the ground on Bolan's heels.

The Beretta 93-R's selector switch already flicked to 3-round bursts, Bolan swept the shadows, left to right. Firing from the hip, feeling the slipstream of hot bullets graze his scalp, the soldier drilled 9 mm Parabellum holes in the chests of the unknown enemy. To Bolan's left flank, coming out of his roll, Grimaldi was already firing .45ACP thunderclaps from his Llama autopistol. Together the two men knocked the shadow gunmen off their feet. Their targets were dead before they hit the ground, but autofire blazed on for a moment before the assault rifles went silent.

Combat senses on full alert, Bolan checked the inky blackness along the front gate, then the parked tractor trailers, luxury vehicles and garbage bins. Holstering his Beretta, the soldier drew his mini-Uzi and cocked the bolt. As far as Bolan could tell, nothing moved on their rear, front or flanks. Side by side the two men sprinted for a door on the platform beyond the loading dock. On the run, Bolan gave the rooftops of the surrounding warehouses one last search, but was unable to spot any watching shadows or snipers.

Clearly all hell had broken loose in the warehouse. It would cover their sudden entry, but there was no telling, Bolan knew, what or whom they would find inside. If there were more gunmen around the perimeter, evacuation could prove touch-and-go. First things first.

Streaking up between two 18-wheelers, Bolan and Grimaldi bounded up onto the dock. Reaching the door, the Executioner tried the handle and found it unlocked. Beyond, the relentless chatter of autofire struck the door. Grimaldi pulled the Uzi subgun off his shoulder, tucking away the Llama. If there were security cameras on the building or its perimeter, they had been hidden from the naked eye.

Someone had come to kill Pinchot, or perhaps get information out of him. There were at least two warring factions inside. With luck, speed and determination, Bolan hoped he and Grimaldi could strike their blind side.

"Follow my lead," Bolan told his friend. "I want a live one, if possible."

Grimaldi nodded.

Bolan flung the door wide. He went in low, Grimaldi high. The racket of autofire sounded as if it came from the far north end of the warehouse. Dim light from naked overhead bulbs shone down on the wide, empty corridor that led to the warehouse proper. In the distance, on the sprint, Bolan caught voices yelling in what he believed was Russian.

Crouching at the end of the corridor, Bolan pinpointed the autofire as coming from beyond the piled crates and massive steel containers. Definitely from the deep north end, the soldier determined. He scanned the catwalks. Glass-encased, roofless cubicles staggered up there, apparently empty.

"I'll take the high ground. You hit them from behind," Bolan told Grimaldi. "Watch yourself."

Grimaldi nodded, but the soldier was already scaling the iron ladder. Bolan had known Grimaldi for what seemed to be a lifetime. Both men knew they could count on each other to not only cover the other's back, but also to accomplish their objective.

Climbing, exposed to potential enemy gunfire but knowing the combatants were engaged in an all-out firefight that would give him critical seconds, Bolan spotted the enemy numbers. At the north edge of the massive warehouse, six men with AK-47s were firing at another group of seven hardmen with automatic weapons. Rising up the ladder, Bolan started to form a strategy.

Then he glimpsed the woman from Colombia.

She stood just inside one of several doorways of the roofless cubicle. As she held back the trigger of a Swiss SG-540 rifle, she shouted orders in Spanish.

Somehow she had escaped into the jungle along the Magdalena River and returned to her masters. It had been a daring hit, seizing the cocaine and aircraft of the enemies, killing many, capturing a few. Who she was and exactly what she was doing in Marseilles didn't matter to the soldier. It was obvious she was in charge, barking orders for her crew to make a move, outflank the Russians. At the moment it looked a standoff between both sides.

Bolan saw two Russians make their move to counter the flanking strategy. Then he spotted René Pinchot. The shipping boss was in bad shape. Though the man's face was a mask of agony, Bolan clearly recognized Pinchot from the intel photos sent from Stony Man Farm.

Hanging upside down, Pinchot was roped by his ankles to another doorway in the same cubicle. He was naked from the waist up, hands bound behind his back, a gag in his mouth. His torso was a bloody mess. What Bolan suspected was Pinchot's security force—five in all, at first glance—were strewed about the warehouse floor in various attitudes of death, machine pistols and mini-Uzis clutched in their fists. Most likely they had greeted the Colombians who had shot first, then strung up Pinchot for torture. Then enter the Russians, disturbing the torture session.

The Spanish woman ran to take up position behind Pinchot, firing her Swiss rifle, screaming at the top of her lungs at her comrades.

Bolan hit the catwalk. He pulled the Beretta and flicked the selector switch to single shot. Below he spotted Grimaldi. Uzi poised to fire, the ace pilot was snaking his way between the steel containers, angling up on the backside of the Russians. Grimaldi was moving hard, nearly in position where the two of them could hit the enemy, high and low.

Bolan came to a spot above the warring factions. He set both mini-Uzi and Beretta on the catwalk, then took and primed both frag grenades. The first steel egg dropped from Bolan's hand. Just as it bounded and rolled up on the rear of the Russian gunners, the Executioner lobbed the second frag grenade.

The first explosion consumed the Russians with roaring fire and shredded them with countless scything steel fragments. Their opposition froze for a moment at the sight of bodies riding a fireball over the crates and steel containers. Confusion turned to screams of agony for the Colombians when the second grenade blew through their ranks.

As expected, there were survivors, a few gunmen who had escaped ground zero, maybe spotted the grenades and made a run for it.

Bolan went to grim work with his Beretta. Sighting down, he cored 9 mm rounds through the skulls of two men moaning and staggering from the smoke. Grimaldi added to the mop-up, his Uzi stuttering away. Holding back on the subgun's trigger, Grimaldi peppered the wounded hardmen with 9 mm lead, tracking on for fleeing Colombians and flinging them in all directions with concentrated sprays of autofire.

The woman and another man were making a hasty retreat for the back exit. In tandem they began to fire up at the catwalk. Lead whined off the steel around Bolan, the structure swaying as the soldier ran from the tracking fire. Triggering the mini-Uzi and Beretta, he sent a staggering, bloodied figure crashing into a pile of crates. He was drawing a bead on the woman and her companion when they burst out the door.

BOLAN AND GRIMALDI converged among the dead.

"The woman's gone," the ace pilot stated. "They were in a car and moving before I hit the door."

While Bolan descended the catwalk, Grimaldi had pursued the enemy outside. A bank of security cameras had been mounted in Pinchot's office. One of the cameras showed a dark luxury vehicle traveling rapidly away from the docks, racing around the far corner of the warehouse.

"I'm sure we'll see her again."

A nod from the Executioner, and Grimaldi took a few steps away to monitor their surroundings.

Muffled gagging sounded from the hanging crimson figure. Bolan hurried to Pinchot. He took his combat knife from its sheath, and, holding the Frenchman's belt, he sliced off the rope and gently lowered the man to the floor. Glancing at Pinchot and the blood pooling around the office doorway and taking a sniff of the pungent stench of rubbing alcohol and gasoline that had been poured into the deep gashes over his face, chest and arms, the soldier suspected the Frenchman wasn't long for the world. Too much blood had been lost, and shock was about to set in.

The smell of burned flesh also struck Bolan's senses. He saw the black-purple lumps that used to be Pinchot's ears. It was a crude but effective form of torture. Maximum pain, while keeping the victim conscious. Whether the Colombians had inflicted this agony on Pinchot for vengeance or information, Bolan didn't know, wasn't even sure how much he cared. The shipping boss was a coconspirator for major importers of narcotics and human flesh. The misery and suffering he had helped to created in the name of a dollar might have easily reached across all of Europe and consumed countless lives.

Bolan pulled the gag out of Pinchot's mouth. The Frenchman's eyes glazed over, rolled around for a moment, then he vomited. His cheek had been slashed to the bone, and his silver hair was crimson from free-flowing blood.

"Pinchot, can you hear me?"

"Y-yes..."

"Sarpries is dead. You're not going to make it, either.

Answer my questions, and I can avenge what happened to you.''

Pinchot's eyes focused on Bolan. "It is you...." He grimaced, crying out in pain. "The one who sank our ship. A lot of people are very interested in you. You, avenge me?" Anger and bitterness appeared to revive Pinchot. "Perhaps I will come back and haunt you...if you do not kill them.... One thing..."

"What?"

"I am a dead man in Marseilles. I have failed...I have talked...you kill me...quick...I answer your questions...."

Bolan didn't give it a second thought. Pinchot had apparently given out information under torture that would cause serious trouble for the men he worked for. Beyond the pain and anger, Bolan spotted a profound sorrow in the Frenchman's eyes. Pinchot, Bolan sensed, was looking to hold on to some last shred of honor, and he was looking to Bolan to give it to him. The soldier knew that all men make choices. All too often, he knew, they were the wrong ones. Men were driven by greed, lust, ambition, and the savage looked to better him- or herself at the expense of others. Even still, when a man faced his own death in the eye, was prepared to make an accounting for his wrong turns, there was honor and a way back to himself.

"Agreed. What happened here?"

"They have come here all...day. Colombians who want to know where the Americans can be found... They demand money owed them...."

"From Calhoun and McBain?"

"Yes. I have to suspect they want to kill them after they get their money. The Russians, they came when the Colombians left…a big, spooky Ivan…scars all over his face…black eyes…friend of the major's…"

Bolan recalled the man he had seen arguing with Calhoun on McBain's villa balcony in Cartagena. An ex-KGB agent?

"I gave…Colombians…directions…phone number to the château where the Americans are. The Americans are nervous…they tell me…to let them know…describe you…I know of this…château…I grew up in the region…."

An idea formed in Bolan's mind. "Give me the phone number."

Pinchot told Bolan the number, and he mentally filed it away.

"Who were the Russians?"

Pinchot gritted his teeth against the pain. "Who knows? Russian Mafia? I have been threatened all day…the Russian spook…here when you called…ordered me to send my men to kill you…think he knew they would…fail… Carreaux's angry…lost money. He called…told the Russian spook to go see him…."

"How long ago?"

"Thirty minutes maybe…before the Colombians returned…just gunned my men down…we did not…stand a chance."

"I want directions to where Carreaux lives," Bolan said, and Pinchot told him.

Curious, Bolan asked, "Who was the woman?"

Pinchot bared his teeth in a strange smile. "Tell me, are you the one who killed Maldonado?"

Bolan had a flash of the instant on the tarmac of the Cali drug lord's private airport when he had shot the king of cocaine kings. "Yes."

"Maldonado was a close business associate with Carreaux, who was approached by Calhoun and the Russian…we have all done business in the past…made fortunes…Carreaux lost his only major supplier…."

"I bleed for him. The woman?"

"The woman is Maria Maldonado…his daughter…by a mistress…."

With everything he had seen and so far learned, with all the players and hidden agendas yet uncovered, Bolan would have been surprised under other circumstances.

At the moment, the schemes of the enemy were secondary. Finding, isolating and destroying them was Bolan's top priority. It looked as if a visit to Pierre Carreaux was next on Bolan's shopping list.

"These men…you destroyed one of the biggest drug deals…ever…they will go to any lengths to kill you…."

"So I've seen."

"Have I answered your questions?"

Bolan drew the silenced Beretta. "Yes."

SVETLANA ZHOLKOVSKY sensed the two Americans were the trouble from Colombia. The way they had killed her backup team near the front gate with such lightning and deadly precision told her they were faced with opposition unlike any she had ever seen. Even still, Petre Kuschka wasn't a man prone to exaggerate or panic. He had said they were dangerous, and they had to be stopped at all costs. Earlier he had given Pinchot his orders and his chance to kill the Americans, but she believed Kuschka already knew the French thugs would fail. She knew he would have seen to it personally, but time was running out in France. Urgent matters of money, men and matériel were waiting to be picked up and moved from Europe, Lebanon and Pakistan. Unfortunately the money might not be on hand to conclude the deals.

Right then her longtime comrade was scrambling to tie up loose ends in Marseilles. Shortly she would join her lover at the beachfront villa of Pierre Carreaux. He was on his way, she knew, to offer the man his only hope of seeing another day. The criminal would hand over a fortune in cash to help further the goals of the Coalition, or the former Spetsnaz troops she had handpicked herself to aid in this emergency would kill anything that even moved on the grounds of the beachfront estate.

Crouched on her haunches, she swept back her long silky blond mane and waited for the two Americans to show. She had removed the radio earpiece, as her ears were still ringing from the deafening explosions that had minutes ago decimated her force. She knew her men were dead. She had watched the Colombian and a comrade leap into a vehicle and speed off into the night. Beneath her black leather trench coat, a 9 mm Makarov was in a shoulder holster. She was supposed to monitor the action, and had attempted to alert Gregor Malaky when the trouble had showed up. But something had gone wrong. Malaky had either been too swept up in the frenzy of the firefight to respond or he had dropped his handheld radio.

Gaze narrowed, her cat green eyes scanned the shipyard from her vantage point on the rooftop of the warehouse next to Pinchot's main building. The shipyard had been under her surveillance all day. Manifests showed there would be no boat traffic for another hour.

All alone at the moment, she seethed. The day had

been lost in tracking, watching, disentangling plots and schemes.

Earlier the Colombians had come and gone, and Petre Kuschka had paid Pinchot a visit to alert him to the trouble they had suffered in Cartagena. When one billion U.S. dollars' worth of cocaine had vanished in fire and smoke, someone had to answer in pain and blood. The Colombians wanted their pound of flesh, and had returned to take it from Pinchot. The Americans were simply another problem, to be solved in short order.

She watched the loading bays in front of the warehouse. As expected, she saw the men roll from the warehouse. Taking her infrared binoculars, she adjusted the focus and branded their faces into her memory.

So they had survived.

As graceful as a cat, she wheeled away from the edge of the warehouse, then unfolded her long, lean frame to its full six feet. She felt a moment's regret that she hadn't brought the SVD Dragunov sniper rifle. It would have been easy to gun down the two Americans with silenced, high-powered bullets while they headed for their vehicle. Perhaps too easy.

In time, she told herself. Over the years as a KGB assassin and a beautiful blonde from the Ukraine, she had been able to go places and maneuver her way toward a target in a manner that her male counterparts couldn't.

It could prove very interesting, she thought, if she managed to get up close and personal with the two Americans.

5

Blood pulsing in his temples, Petre Kuschka choked down his growing anger. Shifting his weight in the wing-back chair and unfolding his legs, the former KGB assassin checked his watch again. They were enjoying a good laugh at his expense. Well, in a few short minutes the fat, balding gangster and his two henchmen, he knew, might die laughing.

Even as they chuckled and glowered at him, the Spetsnaz commandos—flown into Marseilles by his female counterpart—were making their approach, prepared to converge from four points on the gangster's cliff-side mansion. It didn't matter that the Frenchman had an armed security force of at least fifteen men inside the mansion or patrolling the grounds, many of them proved, professional killers and soldiers, according to Coalition intelligence. Never mind the attack dogs, the security cameras.

Kuschka had made his one and only offer, but he had known walking in that the Marseilles boss would never agree to his terms.

Kuschka stared across the massive oak desk at Pierre Carreaux. The boss of Marseilles swirled the whiskey in his glass. With his silk white shirt open to expose dangling jewelry and flabby breasts more suited to a woman than a man, it was difficult for Kuschka to picture the Frenchman as a former leg-breaker and cold-blooded killer who had climbed up the pecking order the hard way to become the most feared, respected and wealthiest gangster in all of Europe.

Their laughter fading, the crackling of flames from the fireplace beside the boss filled the silence. Kuschka glanced at the big goon who stood a few feet away from him. Stripped of his Makarov pistol, Kuschka formed a mental image in his mind of how he would attack and kill the man when the time came. The thug on his flank had a .44 AutoMag in shoulder holster, and he would have to go first. Thug number two, hands clasped in front of him like his comrade, stood beside the desk, twin .357 Magnum pistols holstered for a cross draw. French cowboys, Kuschka thought, watching too many American movies.

Carreaux settled back in his chair and sipped his drink. His eyes cold, he said, "You are perhaps joking, no?"

Kuschka felt his jaw clench, his nostrils flare. Rage ebbed into the familiar icy cold prekill steeling of nerves. He massaged his face, feeling the old scars from flying shrapnel of a war long since lost to ragtag bands of mujahideen, traced with a long finger the jagged, dead flesh on his temple carved there from a long-dead enemy's knife. Finally he smoothed back his silver hair and sucked in a deep breath through his nose. His dark eyes, nearly hidden by bushy black eyebrows, returned the French gangster's penetrating stare.

"I am not a man of humor," Kuschka said. "I prefer to be taken very seriously, Comrade Carreaux."

Carreaux grunted, killed his drink, put the glass down with a thud on his desk. "As I wish to be likewise taken seriously, 'Comrade.' Allow me to understand what you are saying. Feel free to stop me and correct me at any time if I did not hear you right.

"A ship we have successfully used twice before on the same route, loaded with merchandise for which I was supposed to get ten percent, investing my time, money and trouble, was blown up by a fighter jet and sunk to the bottom of the Caribbean. My main source of cocaine is shot dead near his own home. You still owe Maldonado's organization money for which they have come to Marseilles with their killers to get. You and your American friends had some problems overseas in the form of two men, who, you claim, have followed you to my front door. Even worse yet, the Colombians may believe you had something to do with Maldonado's death, and that you and I are connected in this deal. Meaning your troubles have become my troubles. This is not only a fiasco but it is an absolute nightmare. Finally you now tell me, after I have lost my merchandise while out ten million dollars," Carreaux said, glancing, incredulous, at his henchmen and chuckling, "you want fifty million dollars in cash from me."

Carreaux paused, bared his teeth. "Are you insane? Or is this truly a very sick joke?"

"Neither. You heard my proposal. I have offered you a way out and a better life."

"You are insane, then. You want me to be part of this new world you speak of, and all I need to do is hand over fifty million dollars. What new world? Look around you."

Carreaux gestured at his sprawling study. It was complete with giant bar, pool table, bookcases, a whirlpool. There were large oil paintings of the gangster with either one of his four ex-wives, five children or alone, but mostly of Carreaux. The man had built a shrine to himself, Kuschka observed. Elsewhere, divans and other furniture looked as if they belonged in a France of four hundred years ago. Mounted along the walls were ornately carved birds and predators in gold.

"This is just a microscopic piece of my world," Carreaux said. "Those animals you see are made of pure gold. The furniture in this study alone belonged to kings and queens I am sure you never heard of. I have more money than any god a man could pray to. In other words, do you not understand who you are dealing with? I am one of the richest and most powerful men in Europe. I could crush you like an insect!"

"That is precisely why I made you my offer. Out of respect and necessity. We have estimated your net worth far exceeds fifty million dollars."

"I want my money, Kuschka!" Carreaux hammered the desk with a clenched fist. "You are attempting to con me, and I am not one to try to deceive. You blew it, and now you make this insane proposal of giving me my own country to rule! I already rule an entire country—and beyond!"

Kuschka checked his watch. Three minutes and counting.

"Why do you keep looking at your watch?"

The Russian showed Carreaux an odd smile.

"If you would kindly indulge me, Comrade Carreaux. I made a similar offer to other men—shall we say, entrepreneurs—such as yourself. I am merely a soldier in a new war that will soon be fought, a war that will forever change the entire face of the earth and the destiny of humankind. It will be a world in which only the strongest and the smartest will rule. The masses who feed like parasites off the strong, they will become slaves to the rest of us. It is said that one percent of humanity owns fifty percent of the earth's wealth. That number will change soon, and to a staggering degree. With that coming change, a few men will be uplifted as gods, supreme human deities unlike anything the world has ever seen. I see all that you have. Only ask yourself is it enough, is there more? I ask you to imagine, for yourself, the remainder of your life, for your inheritors, a world where your every pleasure and desire is fulfilled with no repercussions whatsoever. In short, to become a god to all men.''

"I already have that, you fool!"

Kuschka held up a restraining hand. "Please. I am speaking of something you cannot even begin to fathom. Since the beginning of time, all men have sought immortality, life everlasting. They crave that more than all the gold in the world, more than all the pleasures of the flesh. I tell you now, the future holds a world in which all natural resources—a small measure of our aims—will be harnessed for their utmost potential. It is merely a means to an end, though, in order to help to create a world where a new species of man will reign, a human prototype superior in every way to the best soldier, the most brilliant scientist, the most gifted artist.

"I am not speaking of robotics or cloning or any other form of genetic engineering. The ones who do not belong with us will be implanted with a computerized chip in their brain, a form of a lobotomy but much more sophisticated, that will make them puppets to our will, allow them to only barter for food and clothing according to their services to us. It is why I have joined forces with the Americans. But there are many other countries, other foreign militaries and intelligence agencies, involved with us. Men of power you would not even consider belonging to such a plan, which will alter the fate of the world. I cannot say more at this time."

Carreaux chuckled. "I believe what you speak of was already attempted by Hitler!"

"Who failed. We will not fail. I only wish to know if you want to be a part of this world. Before you say anything, I will tell you that to create this new world, the old one will have to be torn down. Even the Europe as you know it will not exist in the near future. As we speak, the four elements of such destruction are being produced."

Kuschka reached into his coat pocket and took out a sealed glass tube.

Vicious-sounding laughter poured from the Frenchman's mouth. "This is madness! I should—"

"Should what? Throw me out? Kill me?" Kuschka held up the vial. "In this tube is the most deadly chemical agent ever created. I drop this vial and it breaks, the liquid becomes vapor as it is exposed to oxygen. I can kill all of us in an agonizing, shrieking death in less than thirty seconds. Surely you have heard of the effects of the Ebola virus. Our chemical agent contains the killing effects of the virus, but ten times worse than Ebola. Now, do I have your undivided attention?"

They froze, staring with fear at the vial.

Without warning, Kuschka let the vial fall from his hand. They started to run, but Kuschka sat, utterly still, as the vial shattered on the marble floor. They froze again, appeared startled that Kuschka would sit, immobile, willingly accept a horrible death. Liquid pooled around Kuschka's feet, but no vapor hissed. Carreaux had risen from his chair. The Frenchman glared at Kuschka.

"It is only water," Kuschka said.

"What is the meaning of this game you play?"

"I play no game. Trust me, I do have the real chemical agent at my disposal. As we speak, that very chemical I mentioned has been processed in a mass quantity to be used on a country my superiors have already chosen as a guinea pig."

One last look at his watch and Kuschka saw the attack had begun. He heard a dog barking from somewhere on the grounds. The double doors burst open as the muffled retorts of autofire sounded outside.

A goon with a French MAS assault rifle said, "We are under attack!"

The Russian made his play. The goon beside him was reaching for his weapon when Kuschka, moving with astonishing speed, used his hand like a claw and ripped out the man's throat. Before the blood was even pouring from his victim's ragged hole, Kuschka whipped the AutoMag from the man's holster. As the stunned henchman beside the desk pulled his weapon, Kuschka triggered a thunderous .44 round and blew the Frenchman into the wall. Another henchman, also armed with a French MAS assault rifle, swept into the study but Kuschka greeted them both with a one-two roaring of AutoMag death. As they were launched back into the hallway, Kuschka wheeled and trained the big pistol on Carreaux.

"I see you are no longer laughing."

The Frenchman was shaking in fear as he held his hands in front of him. Beyond the study, Kuschka heard the ceaseless racket of weapons fire, the screams of men taking bullets and dying fast and hard.

"Now, Comrade Carreaux, who, as they say, will get the last laugh?"

THE PALACE of the French boss was under siege. But Bolan had come to the estate on the cliff overlooking the dark expanse of the Mediterranean Sea expecting nothing else. The enemy was jumpy, pointing fingers at each other. Huge sums of money had been lost, plans placed on the backburner. Rage, bitterness, deceit and treachery clearly motivated the enemy here.

It was a mop-up job for the Executioner and Grimaldi before moving on.

Carreaux might have been a small piece of the puzzle, but Bolan had learned enough to know the French boss was involved with the enemies he sought. If the unknown enemy storming the mansion didn't end the Frenchman's reign as boss of bosses, then the Executioner would see to it personally.

Armed with M-16s with attached M-203s, dressed in blacksuits, webbing fitted with spare grenades and clips for the assault rifles, Bolan and Grimaldi swiftly moved on the wrought-iron front gates of the long driveway.

The sedan hidden in a vineyard, the two men had surveyed the mansion and its sprawling grounds from a hillside vantage point, watched the firefight long enough to know they could make their move in a full-frontal assault. The estate was isolated enough from distant, surrounding farmland, a scattered fishing village along the coast, to keep the intense fighting from alerting the locals and drawing the police to the cliff. At least, long enough for Bolan and Grimaldi to strike the warring factions from the blind side.

Again Bolan was looking to shave the enemy numbers until he could get to Calhoun and McBain. With any luck all his enemies would be gathered here. But he wouldn't cling to false hope.

Château Pyrenees was next on the search-and-destroy

list. Bolan suspected Calhoun and McBain and their Russian counterparts were keeping the troops spread out.

They covered the short distance across the stone bridge. The relentless chatter of autofire was tapering off, and the cries of the wounded were fading rapidly.

But it was still enough noise to cover their swift and deadly entrance.

The front gate was a six-foot affair both men scaled with ease. Security cameras were mounted on the gate, staggered at intervals along the stone wall ringing the compound, not that it mattered any longer.

Side by side, Bolan and Grimaldi sprinted up the driveway, taking in the armed shadows scurrying around the grounds, skirting the dead and firing at other armed figures along the marble-columned front entrance. Bolan gave the order for Grimaldi to peel off to his flank and open fire at will.

Sliding in behind the trees lining the driveway, Bolan picked out a group of four gunmen with blazing Kalashnikovs, who had taken cover behind several luxury vehicles. The Executioner triggered his M-203.

"FOR EACH TIME you dared to laugh at me," Kuschka snarled, "I laugh back with one bullet!"

"I will give you money!" Carreaux screamed. "I have five million in U.S. dollars in the safe...."

Kuschka triggered the .44 AutoMag. The first round blew a hole in Carreaux's upper chest, near his right shoulder. The Frenchman yelled in agony, spun, hit his knees.

"I believe that was for the first time."

Another peal of thunder, the slug shearing off a

chunk of the Frenchman's right thigh. Carreaux crumpled onto his back.

"I do not take rejection lightly."

Consumed with fury, Kuschka moved around the desk, sighting down the AutoMag. Outside he heard the din of weapons fire closing on the front of the mansion. The night belonged to his Spetsnaz commandos. He stared down at Carreaux, who looked like a beached whale to him. Two more roaring retorts from the AutoMag, and Carreaux was pinned to the marble floor, with one shot to the other shoulder and leg.

"I leave you now, Comrade, to die, not like a man, but as a worm I have crushed."

Kuschka spun on his heel. He was satisfied with how the attack was going. He allowed himself a moment of pride that the attack outside and his utter destruction of the Frenchmen in the study had gone so well. It reminded him of the old days when he killed for the KGB. Strike when a target least expected it.

Kuschka smiled, and was stripping one of the dead men of his assault rifle when the mansion was rocked by two explosions from the front. None of his commandos was armed with that kind of firepower.

IT WAS AS IF the sky fell on them, the whole night exploding on the enemy out of nowhere. No sooner had Bolan and Grimaldi blown the luxury vehicles apart with a double-punch of decimating fireballs than both warriors reloaded the breech with a 40 mm grenade. Again they unloaded the hell-bombs on muffled crunching sounds, the warheads sizzling toward approaching hardmen downrange. Even before the second fiery impacts, they reloaded, fired again. A line of thundering explosions lit the driveway and the front of the mansion.

Bolan didn't want to waste one critical second in getting bogged down in an extended firefight.

It didn't appear as if he had to worry about that.

Bodies were sailing in all directions, warped debris flying into the front of the mansion, blasting through windows. Figures staggering from the smoke from the columned front entrance, Bolan and Grimaldi moved out. Triggering their M-203s on the run, they mowed down wounded enemy with sweeping bursts of 5.56 mm autofire.

Cautious, checking his fire as they whirled, dropped and rolled down the steps, Bolan scanned the sprawling grounds. Bodies littered the manicured lawn from the east and west, both man and animal. Bolan wasn't about to trust first appearances.

Far to his flank, he spotted Grimaldi, M-16 poised, shadowing up the steps. Checking his rear, finding nothing moving among the smoking, flaming ruins of vehicles and a few enemy dead torched by the fireballs, Bolan hit the steps, moved past a sprawled body. Ahead he watched the smoking rubble of the massive front doors, which had been blown to matchsticks by a 40 mm grenade. He suspected the Russians had sealed the mansion with a pincer attack, believed there were still gunmen somewhere inside the building.

Crackling fire in his ears, Bolan nearly topped the steps when sudden movement blurred in the smoking maw ahead, and cut loose with autofire.

THE ROCKY HILL north of the killing grounds provided a perfect vantage point for Svetlana Zholkovsky. Moving away from her Lincoln Towncar, she dropped to a knee on the edge of a precipice overlooking a vineyard.

She lifted the infrared binoculars to her eyes, adjusted the focus and took in the Frenchman's compound.

The Americans had struck again, with swift and deadly accuracy. They had used grenades, hitting her force from the blind side.

She was too little too late. Almost.

At worst she had been ten minutes behind the two Americans, tailing them from a distance down the coastal highway. They had lucked out, stumbling onto the attack on the Frenchmen, gaining advantage on the Spetsnaz commandos while they attacked the mansion.

Two critical items were on the ground beside her at the moment. One was the handheld radio she would use in a minute to contact Petre Kuschka. Judging the fires from the explosions that had utterly destroyed both man and machine, she worried for a moment if he was even still alive. She hoped he was still inside the mansion, knew the attack strategy was to move in on the compound from four points on the compass while he made the life-or-death offer to Carreaux. A few commandos had to be alive still, having hit the mansion from the back. The Americans hadn't won here yet.

Then, panning the front entrance to the mansion, she spotted her targets. Angry that the bulk of their commandos appeared dead, she felt more than sufficient motivation to kill.

She picked up the SVD Dragunov sniper rifle and slapped the 10-round detachable box magazine into the weapon. Another quick look through the binoculars and she saw the Americans moving up the front steps. One of them was securing cover behind a pillar, maybe a dozen yards from the taller of the two.

She chambered a 7.62 mm round and sighted into the infrared PSO-1 scope. Distance to target moving up the steps was roughly one hundred meters. Allowing for the soft breeze blowing off the Mediterranean, distance and downward trajectory, she adjusted the scope and snugged the stock against her shoulder.

It had been at least four years since she had sniped a target. But her training with the rifle from KGB marksmen who believed no woman could handle the 4.4 kilogram rifle, and her stubborn determination to prove them wrong over the years came back. Grim pride filled her.

She curled her finger around the trigger, took up slack as she drew a bead on the back of the taller American's head.

6

Barely escaping their tracking barrage of lead, Bolan sprinted to cover behind a pillar. Out of the corner of his eye, he spotted Grimaldi, hugging the face of the building, plucking a hand grenade from his webbing. The Executioner primed a fragmentation grenade, wheeled low around the pillar and lobbed the steel egg with an underhand motion, in sync with Grimaldi, as lead whined off stone above his head. Voices were shouting in Russian beyond the soldier's position, though he couldn't determine how many Russians were inside.

Innocents were inside being slaughtered. Moments ago he had also heard screaming and shouting of women from somewhere close, just inside the mansion. Long bursts of autofire then rattled the air, and screams were silenced. Obviously the Russians weren't leaving anyone alive.

Then Bolan found a new threat charging his flank. The bloody shadow made a sudden rush for the soldier, bounding up the steps. In the wavering firelight, Bolan saw that the man's face was shredded by shrapnel. It was the commando knife, poised high over the enemy's head, that snared the Executioner's undivided attention.

The frag bombs blew, one after the other, overwhelming the din of weapons fire. Wheeling, the enemy nearly on top of him, Bolan hurled his M-16 upward. He blocked the descending knife, jarred to the bone.

The horribly wounded man was consumed with pain or blind rage, snarling in Bolan's face, his eyes lit with savage determination. The enemy spun with the defensive maneuver as the soldier twisted, his rifle hooked to the arm wielding the knife. Shoving his adversary away with his M-16 to draw a bead on him, Bolan stumbled into the pillar. As he brought up the M-16, the top of the man's head exploded.

Rolling thunder washed over the compound.

Bolan was up and already moving around the pillar, heading for the smoking ruins of the doorway as more distant thunder sounded from somewhere beyond the compound. Ducking, the soldier heard the projectile screaming off stone from the cover he had just left. He joined Grimaldi at the debris and told his friend, "We've got a sniper out there."

A quick search of the compound was fruitless. There was no time to pinpoint a muzzle-flash, which would expose the sniper's position. To stay put meant certain death.

Side by side, both men rushed past the sprawled bodies.

Clearing the smoke, Bolan found the living room and the winding spiral staircase, which led to the upstairs, littered with bodies. One look at the unarmed victims and Bolan knew they were either family members or friends of Carreaux, or servants.

Cautiously moving into the living room, with Grimaldi peeling off beside a large divan, Bolan looked around but found no sign of the enemy. If any Russians had survived, he knew they had gone out the back door.

BOLAN STOOD OVER the dying boss. The glazed look in the Frenchman's eyes cleared a little with anger and bitterness.

Grimaldi stood guard at the doorway.

Carreaux was soaked with blood from his wounds.

"What happened here, Carreaux?"

"Bastard Russian…"

"I need a name."

"Kuschka…KGB…or former…should have never trusted him…"

It was too late for regrets. What Bolan now learned about an American-Russian alliance only added more confusion to a growing list of questions about the enemy's agenda.

Carreaux gnashed his teeth in agony, his eyes rolling back in his head. "My family…daughters…grandchildren were here.…"

"Kuschka killed them, Carreaux. They didn't deserve to die the way they did, but you share a lot of the responsibility for what happened to them."

The French boss cursed Bolan.

"You want revenge, talk to me."

"Why should I? You are the bastard that blew my deal."

"I'm the one, but I had a little bit of help from a friend. Help me understand what happened here, and I'll find the ones responsible."

Talk of revenge appeared to revive a flickering of light into the Frenchman's eyes. "Who do you want revenge for?"

"It doesn't matter. Just consider it done. What do you know about Kuschka's involvement with former American military men?"

"He...Calhoun...McBain...the Americans...your own military...you judge me..."

"I don't judge you. You've judged yourself."

"They...are worse than what...you think of me. I only give others what they want. They are... killers...talked about...a new world...crazy...is going to unleash some plague..."

"Against who?"

"Didn't say—some...lesser people, he called them. Third World..." Choked laughter erupted from his mouth. "Nazi talk from a Russian...world...change... they...deceived me...."

"It's a tough life."

Bolan stared, hard-eyed, at the dying man. If what he just heard was true, then he believed that the mass suicide terrorist attack in Manhattan would only prove a small measure of what the enemy had planned.

The Frenchman's head lolled to one side. The boss was dead. There was nothing more Bolan could do or achieve here.

"Sarge, we need to go. If there were any of them left, they're gone."

Quickly Bolan and Grimaldi retraced their way to the front-entrance ruins.

"Use the woods to make it back?" Grimaldi asked.

Bolan nodded. "If we can get a fix on the sniper," he said, loading the breech of his M-203, "we'll hit him and keep moving. If nothing else, we can keep him pinned down long enough to get back."

They made a run for the pillars. Bolan scanned the dark hills to the north and spotted a vehicle moving along the ridgeline, maybe a hundred yards away. If their sniper was pulling out, Bolan would know soon enough.

"Let's do it," the soldier said.

Sprinting down and off the steps, the two men then angled for the woods that lined the driveway. When they drew no fire, Bolan knew the sniper was gone.

As they put the killing ground behind them, Bolan pondered Carreaux's revelation. Whatever the enemy was planning, Bolan suspected it was a horror beyond anything he had yet experienced. He had seen the effects of biological and chemical warfare in countless hellgrounds. But he knew this enemy had the money, connections and will to unleash something so potentially devastating the entire fate of humankind could be hanging in the balance.

In the Pyrenees

THE HARD PROBE was meant to size the enemy force, but that was only for starters.

As Bolan swiftly made his way up the rocky slope on the northern foothills, he was going in to deliver a grim message to all adversaries gathered in the mountain château and shave the numbers a little more, if nothing else. Skill, experience, daring and determination carried Bolan through the night. He was fully loaded with hardware in the event it all went to hell. Togged in a blacksuit, he carried a Remington 700 sniper rifle across a shoulder, a combat knife in an ankle sheath and frag grenades fixed to his webbing. The .44 Magnum Desert Eagle rode on his hip. Threading the sound suppressor to the Beretta 93-R, Bolan headed for the ridge.

A quick look over his shoulder revealed the Bell JetRanger, piloted by Grimaldi, fading to the north, angling away from the sleepy village of Beaumont Chalis.

Hitting the button on his radio headset, Bolan spoke into the mike.

"Striker to Skywatcher, come in, Skywatcher."

"Skywatcher here, Striker."

"I'm clear so far. Three hundred yards to target."

"Our satellite recon hasn't failed us yet, Striker," Grimaldi added. "Thirty minutes to deliver the message on your end and evacuate."

"Make the call from your end in fifteen. I want to see if anything comes out of the hornet's nest. Confirm."

"That's affirmative. Good luck. I sure would have rather brought along the other bird for this one."

"Not yet," Bolan said, knowing Grimaldi was referring to his preference for the AH-64 Apache gunship. "I'd rather not tip our hand until I get that face-to-face with the general."

"I know we discussed it, and I've always trusted your judgment, but I really don't think the man will just hand himself over to us."

"I'm counting on some chest-thumping more than anything else. If he's true to form, has sold himself over to the other side for money, then maybe I can make him swagger a little."

"I hope he comes running. If he has a big mouth and wants to bluster about how strong the other team is, we may find out exactly what they're planning. Biological warfare scares the hell out of me."

"I'm on the clock. Start counting off now. Over and out."

Bolan severed radio contact and moved out. Thirty minutes until pickup on the ridgeline. It could prove an eternity.

His night-vision goggles on, Bolan scanned the craggy ridge above. Through the grayish green tint of his goggles, he found nothing but stone and boulder up there. That didn't mean he wouldn't encounter sentries along the way. In fact he was counting on it.

It had been several long grueling hours to get to this next phase of the hunt. Swift but cautious flight, and a little bit of luck, had steered them from the flaming remains of Carreaux's estate, back to the airfield northeast of Marseilles. As either fate or luck had it, there had been no run-in with French authorities. The soldier figured the police had more than enough to deal with in the city proper before moving onto the late boss's compound. A short flight by LearJet from the outskirts of the city, and Bolan and Grimaldi had touched down at the base in the remote wilderness of the Pyrenees.

Alone now, in the dark, braving the cold mountain air, Bolan climbed hard. He searched the ground ahead, mindful of moss-covered rock, his eyes peeled for anything that looked like a booby trap. Even still, he figured the enemy would be smarter than to lay mines or any other form of lethal trap along the mountainside, which would see climbers, tourists, possibly even a wandering shepherd or villager. The Pyrenees stretched 270 miles, from the Mediterranean Sea all the way to the Bay of Biscay on the Atlantic edge, and under other circumstances Bolan would have marveled at the awesome majesty of the mountain chain that divided France from Spain.

But this was no nature hike.

The strike point was situated in the foothills of the granite peaks towering above the soldier in the distance. The snow-covered peak, shaped by time and nature into a spear point, was Bolan's guiding landmark.

How and why McBain had landed a château in the rugged wilderness, due south of Lourdes, was a mystery

Stony Man Farm had yet to resolve. Back at the temporary command post, Bolan had radioed Hal Brognola and brought him up to speed. The big Fed had information involving a new international bank called the World Bank Center. Its head office was in Munich, and one of its founders was Max Tielig. McBain was a major depositor and stockholder in the World Bank Center.

Tielig was on hold at the moment.

Bolan made the ridgeline. Below, nestled on a precipice overlooking a valley, he saw the lit compound marking the château. Lifting the NVD goggles up, he took his infrared binoculars and scanned the target site, adjusting the lens to the two-hundred-yard distance. There was a courtyard, filled to capacity with Jeeps, Land Rovers and four-wheel-drive trucks. According to satellite photos, there was only one dirt road that wound through the valley to the west, leading right to the château. A low stone wall ringed the compound. An executive-style chopper was grounded on the courtyard.

Patrolling the grounds, Bolan counted six sentries, armed with either SMGs or assault rifles. Another search of the premises produced a group of figures, gathered around a long table beyond the window. From the giant window of that room, two men with weapons slung around their shoulders were staring out at the courtyard. Suddenly Bolan saw one of the sentries out front talking into a handheld radio. A moment later the sentry was gesturing at the ridgeline where Bolan was positioned. A lookout had either spotted the chopper or Bolan's ascent, or the enemy had radar inside the château that had picked up the helicopter.

Either way, three armed figures moved away from the compound, headed Bolan's way.

The soldier readjusted his NVD goggles. Below, the

ground sloped away in strewed boulders and footpaths. There wasn't much by way of shelter in trees or brush, but he would find something to cover himself while he went to grim work.

The Executioner moved out to meet the enemy.

One last check of his chronometer, and he saw he had nearly eaten up the allotted fifteen minutes. Grimaldi was about to make the call that would change someone's immediate future.

7

All of them had become like hunted animals.

For what felt like an eternity, that was the singular, cold and enraging thought that consumed Ben Calhoun. Several terrifying visions flashed without prompting or reason through his mind. First a fish on a hook, reeled in, skinned alive with a large knife, sunlight glinting off its blade. Then a deer prancing through the woods, drilled through its heart with an arrow. Finally a charging bull, stuck like a massive pin cushion with the matador's swords, lumbering and snorting in death throes, then dropping at his slayer's feet.

Calhoun felt himself shake with anger and fear, and he shoved the ugly images out of his mind with sheer will. *He* hunted men and killed them or, at worst, knew who his enemies were, could look over his shoulder and see them coming, prepared to eliminate the threat. What had happened to them in the States and then in Colombia was something entirely new, frightening even. A relentless warrior with no name—an avenging hand of God, it seemed—that struck at will, appeared to know their next move even before they did.

He watched as Kuschka slammed the cellular phone on the long knight's table. Undoubtedly more bad news. As the Russian stood at the head of the table, the scars on his temples appeared to pulse like squirming worms as he stared with ill-concealed fury around the dining hall.

"The Colombians are on their way here," the former KGB assassin announced. "That was Maldonado's daughter. To understate the matter, she is extremely upset. I would have to assume she is looking for more from us than just the money owed them after the killing of her father."

Calhoun clenched his jaw. To a large extent, he was responsible for their present crisis. What had begun in New York as an operation to assassinate a senator who may have exposed him had spiraled downward into a nightmare none of them were able to awake from.

Nervous, smoothing back his iron gray hair with his one good hand, the former Special Forces major avoided Kuschka's stare by looking around the table. He flexed his other hand, stiff and sore from stitches. The injured hand was wrapped with gauze. But the pain in the hand, shooting up his arm like an electric charge, was a constant reminder of the horror and rage he had felt before he had crushed a glass into his palm. The news their drug shipment was being obliterated by a fighter jet to sink to the bottom of the Caribbean had been too much to bear.

Now they were faced with dire repercussions for the loss of the drugs and the ship. A little over twenty-four hours had passed since the disaster, but it seemed as if it were just moments ago. The voice of the ship's captain bellowing over the radio—as explosions rocked the deck and the hull—seemed frozen in Calhoun's mind. Of course, reinforcements had been radioed ahead to help tackle the impending disaster he knew would follow them to Europe.

When landing at the private airport north of the small

French village, Calhoun had been greeted by his own reinforcements. Kuschka had also radioed ahead while flying with him over the Atlantic for a backup team to be flown to France. Calhoun had twenty armed men while the Russian had another ten grim-faced, silent men with AK-47s who had been promptly moved into McBain's mountain château.

While waiting for Kuschka to take care of business in Marseilles, Calhoun, McBain, their own American force and the Russians had waited with clearly frayed nerves. Calhoun couldn't decide if he was a prisoner of the Russians, awaiting execution upon further disaster, or if he was still on the same team. The Colt .45ACP was on the table, within easy reach. If someone made a play, he would take out as many of the Russians as possible before he bought it. He could count on his own men to open fire with their Ingrams, Uzis and Heckler & Koch MP-5 subguns in the blink of an eye. He hoped it didn't come to that. The situation was salvageable. Too much remained to be done. Plans for the immediate future had long since been set. The Coalition was counting on them. Of course, word of their present dilemma had reached their superiors, who would have contacted Kuschka and told him how to proceed. Undoubtedly their superiors wanted them all to exercise damage control.

It was less than fifteen minutes since Kuschka, the blond mystery woman—who now sat near the head of the table—and three Spetsnaz commandos had landed in their helicopter on the courtyard. And still Calhoun wasn't privy to what had happened in Marseilles. Judging the cold rage in Kuschka's dark eyes, he suspected a fiasco had taken place.

Either way, Sparrow and Sampson, monitoring the

radar communications bank beyond the table, had confirmed that less than a minute ago an aircraft had flown near the compound, then banked off to the west. The waiting was over. The problem, Calhoun knew, had followed them to what was supposed to be a safehouse in the rugged isolation of the Pyrenees.

McBain, chomping on a cigar, scowled at Calhoun from across the table. "Nobody had this number except Pinchot. He gave us up. Hell, the man must have drawn them a map!"

"It would certainly appear so," Kuschka said.

The blond woman spoke up, her voice cold with controlled anger. "Pinchot is dead. Carreaux is dead. We have no more ties or loose ends in Marseilles. Unfortunately we have lost many good Spetsnaz commandos to two men. Whatever the trouble that has followed us from America to Colombia has arrived in France. I saw both men in Marseilles. I lost a team of commandos to these men at Pinchot's shipyard."

"And only myself and three other commandos escaped the battle at the French gangster's compound. Forgive my poor manners," Kuschka said. "This is Comrade Zholkovsky. She is here to assist me in curtailing the crisis with which we are faced."

"We're taking orders from her?" McBain growled, blowing smoke.

"If necessary," Kuschka replied. "I hope no one has a problem with that."

Zholkovsky flashed an angry look at Calhoun. "It is time to eliminate the dogs that are nipping at our heels. If not, the next two steps of our mission will be seriously jeopardized."

"He's here. You know that, don't you?" Calhoun said, not caring who was giving the orders.

"I have three men, right now, going out to the ridge-line where the aircraft was detected on radar," Kuschka informed.

"What about my people?" Calhoun asked. "We're sitting on our hands. We just wait here while he makes his way down to us? You've already seen what this individual is capable of."

"Indeed, I have. We have other grave problems to also contend with."

McBain chomped on his cigar. "The Colombians. What are you saying—when they get here, we just kill them?"

Kuschka showed them all a strange smile. "Precisely."

Calhoun heaved a breath. During the flight to France, they had been briefed on the next two phases of the Coalition's objectives. Beyond France, the next step was getting to Munich, securing transportation to Lebanon, and funds from Tielig. Easier said than done, he knew, since the German had invested heavily in the drug shipment, lost his part of the deal, not to mention an entire ship and crew. The next phase involved delivery of a chemical-weapons shipment to terrorists in Lebanon. The shipment of chemical weapons had arrived two days earlier in Munich, was being held at Tielig's airfield. The German wasn't even aware of the potential holocaust he was sitting on. Again, Calhoun didn't know the full details of the arrangement between Tielig and Kuschka. He suspected Tielig was now in so deep, that he had no choice but to go with the Russian's program.

"Major," Kuschka said, "order three of your men to go with my commandos as backup."

Calhoun looked at three of his grizzled vets. They

were seated beside the giant, shaved-head Augustly. He would have preferred sending Augustly as part of the three-man team, but he wanted his fastest and meanest gunman there in the room beside him.

"Longwall, Jameson, Custis, move out," the former Special Forces major ordered. They hauled in their subguns and swiftly left the room. "What's the story on that aircraft?"

The short, muscular Sparrow looked from the radar bank and said, "It landed, it would appear, sir, about five miles west of the town."

Grunting, Calhoun looked at the two Russians standing at the long bay window. They were scanning the dark, jagged ridgeline beyond the château through field glasses. Instinct made him wonder who was watching whom at the moment.

"Now, about our immediate future objectives in Germany," Kuschka began. "You know of the shipment that arrived from South Africa to Tielig's airport. It contains the chemical weapon manufactured by our scientists—"

Suddenly the cellular rang. Tension knifed through the dining hall as all eyes fell on Kuschka, who hesitated, then snapped up the phone. "Yes?" A pause, the Russian's expression turning grim a moment later. "What? Who is this?"

Calhoun tensed, found the big Russian staring at McBain with a dark look on his scarred face.

"Can you put this on a speaker, General?"

"By the radar," McBain said, puzzled.

The order was passed on, and the speaker came to life with a voice Calhoun had never heard, but suspected it was their nemesis.

"McBain, listen carefully to me. Two hours, General.

You will go to Beaumont Chalis. There's a café that will be open then, on the north end of the town."

"Who is this?" McBain barked.

"Who I am is not important. You will meet a man in black inside the café. I don't expect you to come alone, but bring no more than one man. I'll give you the details then about your future. Whether you live or die will be up to you."

"What the hell is—"

The connection died over the speaker with a soft buzzing before Sparrow turned off the speaker.

Looking at McBain, Kuschka nodded, said, "It appears as if we might have an opening for a solution to our crisis."

"By sending me down there as bait?" McBain asked.

"He said no more than one man. That one man," Kuschka said, "will be me."

"We can't afford a shoot-out in that town," Calhoun argued. "I'm aware enough bribes have been handed out to local officials, but we didn't buy off the whole town."

"Comrade, one of our men just went down!"

Calhoun was looking toward the Russians by the window. They were under attack by the mystery man.

"Two more just went down!"

In the next instant Calhoun saw the window shatter and watched, stunned, as the binoculars and entire head of the Russian exploded. Before he could even blink his eyes or rise from his chair, Calhoun saw the second Russian make a run for cover only to be blown off his feet and hurled straight for the table.

THE GRIM MESSAGE there was no place for the enemy to run or hide was being driven home with a deadly touch by Bolan.

With the silenced Beretta 93-R, the soldier had first taken out the three-man recon team. Catching them out in the open, maybe thirty yards down the slope, he cut loose with the Beretta on 3-round-burst mode for insurance, leaving them sprawled below his concealment point behind a boulder.

The Executioner then got busy with his sniper rifle. The two figures standing, side by side, inside the large window and surveying the perimeter through field glasses became his next targets. With the 5-round detachable box magazine already in place, a 7.62 mm NATO round chambered, Bolan lined up the first head behind the field glasses in the infrared scope. He adjusted the distance through the scope, allowed for downward trajectory and the wind at his back, took up slack on the trigger, squeezed and blew the man's head off.

Shifting the rifle and cocking the bolt action, he lined up the second target in the crosshairs of the scope. This would prove a tougher shot, as the second man began a dash from the jagged teeth of the shattered window. Bolan gave the target some lead, then caressed the trigger. The big gun thundered in Bolan's fists, the soldier riding out the recoil. The projectile caught target number two between the shoulder blades, lifting him off his feet and hurling him toward the figures scrambling from the long knight's table.

Judging the number of vehicles packed in the courtyard, Bolan figured a small army, maybe forty to fifty enemy guns, was in the compound. A glance at his chronometer and he knew Grimaldi had made the call.

Through his scope he picked out a target, scurrying from near a Jeep, angling for the wall. The Executioner loosed a round that caught the figure in the chest and flung him back into the vehicle.

Voices shouting from the courtyard washed up over Bolan's position. He figured someone was giving the orders for the hardmen to move out. The enemy, though, took up positions behind the front wall, reluctant to make the dash across the open ground leading to the first series of boulders.

A searchlight flared on from the west edge of the courtyard. The beam began to rake the hillside.

Bolan lined up the sights on the searchlight as its beam swung his way. He triggered a 7.62 mm round that shattered the glass in a spray of sparks. In the dark now, the gunners in the compound hugged their positions beyond the front wall.

The soldier waited for a target to show. Three figures slid over the wall a few heartbeats later. Chambering the last round, Bolan fired. Downrange the 7.62 mm projectile, traveling at 850 meters per second, crucified a figure into the wall, as hardmen cut loose on Bolan. Bullets whined off stone, but far to his right flank. They were spraying the area, hoping for a lucky shot. Without the searchlight Bolan knew he stood a good chance of making it back to the ridgeline. He had thrown enough chaos and confusion among the ranks, that perhaps the entire mountainside seemed to be hurling death their way.

Even still, it was touch and go. Dead men were sprawled near his position, and the enemy would surely pinpoint the sound of the rifle's thunder.

He ejected the spent magazine and slapped home a fresh clip into the sniper rifle. It was maybe an eighty-yard hike back to the ridgeline. Boulders were staggered up the slope, here and there. There was a gully, though, tracking up the slope, that Bolan had found on his way down. It would have to cover his path back to his evacuation point.

Below, the soldier found the enemy scuttling up the hill. Slipping his NVD goggles over his eyes, he took two frag grenades, armed them both. The distance to the advancing enemy was roughly fifty yards and closing, on a straight line, right beneath him. He hurled one steel egg after the other down the slope as lead stitched the rocky ground, still to his flank.

He was already up and rapidly climbing the slope when the explosions rocked the air. Screams of pain assaulted his ears as he hurried on.

Return fire ceased for a full half minute as Bolan gained distance. Pumping his arms and legs as hard as he could, he dropped into the gully. He was covered for the time being, but the gully would only offer cover for maybe half the distance to the ridge.

He checked his watch. Five minutes remained before Grimaldi showed.

Then, suddenly, he heard the bleat of the rotor blades, just beyond the ridge. Moments later he saw the dark bulk of the chopper rise above him, hovering.

Bolan hustled up the gully as autofire cut loose in the distance behind him. He patched through to Grimaldi. "I'm right below you, Jack. Thirty yards and closing."

"I'll hold my position. I've got maybe twenty guns moving away from the front wall, but they're out of effective firing range for the moment."

Bolan charged up the incline, hit the slope running. Autofire rattled the air behind him. The sound of lead ricocheting off stone pumped more adrenaline through his veins as he bolted for the chopper, crouched and forged into the rotor wash. He didn't look back as he reached the fuselage doorway, opened it and hurled himself into the cabin. As soon as he hit the floor, he felt the chopper lifting, angling away from the ridge.

Standing, he saw Grimaldi look over his shoulder.

"You're early," Bolan said.

"As soon as I made the call, I had a feeling things were going to heat up."

"If McBain shows, they'll heat up even more."

"And if he doesn't?"

Bolan moved into the cockpit, stared out through the Plexiglas as black sky swept into sight. "Either way, it's your show next time we hit the mountain."

8

Seated in the last booth of the small café, Bolan sipped his coffee. It was just after dawn, the first rays of sunlight washing over the stained-glass windows of the establishment. Through a hooded stare, the soldier watched as the former five-star general walked through the door, spotted him, then moved his way.

Bolan wore his wireless minimike, fixed inside the lapel of his coat. Mug to his lips, he said, "He's in."

Watching the meet site from the east hills that overlooked the sprawling farmland and wine country, Grimaldi answered. "Still just the one vehicle out front. One guy sitting on the driver's side. So far, only two bad guys came to town."

Bolan kept vigilance on the front door. It appeared, at least on the surface, the enemy had done what he had instructed. Still they could be laying a trap. Beneath his coat Bolan was ready to draw either the mini-Uzi from its special shoulder holster, or the Beretta or the Desert Eagle at the first eyeblink of trouble.

Bolan looked over the surroundings for the meet. The place had a medieval feel and look about it, with the stained-glass windows, pewter mugs and plates, everything solid oak or stone, the wizened faces of local men and women who eked out a hardscrabble existence. But this was old Basque country, after all. It was timeless land that had seen the conquering armies of Caesar and Hannibal, the savaging of invading barbarian tribes of the Vandals and Visigoths. Like the stone homes, stretching away in haphazard patterns where shepherds and animals meandered the countryside, the villagers were a sturdy, if not solemn people. If the firefight up the mountain had alerted any villagers or local authorities, Bolan hadn't spotted any sign on the drive to the village. No roadblocks, no uniformed police, no aerial surveillance. If it was pure luck they had escaped a run-in with French authorities, then it seemed to be holding so far.

From behind the wooden counter, the short, white-bearded proprietor glanced at Bolan. He looked suspicious for a moment, then went back to pouring coffee for the assorted customers, mostly men in wool jackets and berets, eating breakfast, smoking and talking in low tones to one another.

McBain slid his heavy bulk into the booth, across from Bolan. The man looked angry and scared, but Bolan could well understand his predicament. He had the enemy running, and he wasn't about to stop until they were trampled into the mountainside. The Executioner spotted the bulge beneath McBain's wool coat, then looked the man dead in the eye.

"So, you're the one pissing on our parade," McBain said.

Bolan waited while the proprietor approached. "Something for you, *monsieur?*" he asked McBain.

"No. Just some quiet time with my friend here."

"Very well." The owner nodded, throwing Bolan and McBain a look, then moved off.

"I see you're covered," McBain said, looking at Bolan's earpiece. "So am I, just in case you think you're here to arrest me."

"I'm not."

"I didn't think so."

"Why, McBain?"

The ex-general studied Bolan for a long moment. "I'm reaching into my coat for a cigar. You don't mind, do you?"

"Go for it."

Bolan waited while McBain fished out the cigar, lighted it with a butane lighter.

McBain slid an ashtray in front of him. "I suppose you're asking me why I spent years handing over intelligence on CIA covert operations in the lower Americas and Eastern Europe to either the drug cartels or the KGB."

"I've already got that much. O'Malley's dead."

"I'm aware of that."

"But he helped put me in the right direction."

"So, his death wasn't for nothing. O'Malley was naive, and blind patriotism's been dead for three decades. He took down a few good friends of mine, but he couldn't get close enough. The man had to fall. It was both for revenge and survival."

Briefly Bolan thought of the late senator. The man's Long Island estate, which had been turned into a killing ground by a suicide attack force, had been the launch point for Bolan's campaign. It had only been a few days earlier, another continent, but it seemed as if he had been chasing an elusive enemy for an eternity.

"Politicians," McBain began, blowing a thick cloud of smoke, "even if they are former military, don't live in the real world. They're more interested in getting reelected and keeping a cush life instead of finding answers to real problems. But it's still about power—who has it, who doesn't.''

"So, tell me what the real world is to you, McBain.''

"Go back up that mountain and you'll find out. You're good, but you've gotten lucky so far. Next time we'll be ready for you, and we all know there will be a next time.''

"That only seems logical.''

"Right. I'm not sure who you work for, but I know Uncle Sam has more than a few, uh, black-ops teams and specialists who have carte blanche to do whatever the hell it is they please, while our government looks the other way. Killing heads of state, dictators, guns for drugs, whatever, all in the name of democracy—I know all the games. You one of them?''

"I'm not about that. And what you said is old news.''

"Not if the American public really knew the full details of the awful truth. Fact is, our government has been busy toppling and destabilizing Third World countries for at least thirty years. Fact is, our government holds its own masses in either contempt or fear. I've had more than one conversation with men of power in Washington who've said things from the heart that would have them flying out of office on their butts. It's all a game of grab-ass, taking whatever's left of the good life before the next guy gets it. We give them social programs, build shopping malls to keep them fed and amused, but it's only a matter of time before America becomes a police state. Crime and drugs, broken families, total disrespect and disregard for the law, they've reached something of epidemic proportions.''

"I'm not here for a social dissertation. And there are still a few good people left who keep it going.''

"Really? Well, bear with me. America, like the rest

of the world, so-called free or otherwise, is in a state of controlled chaos, but it's all a time bomb waiting to blow. Why? It's the same thing that's happened throughout history, with the gap between the rich and the poor ever widening, but nature dictates certain laws. Only so much food, so much raw material, so much of anything to sustain life. In America, as is the case across the world, the haves are slowly but surely being consumed by the have-nots. Something drastic, never before done in the history of the world, has to happen to set it right again. You see, the powers that be, they know Armageddon is only a matter of time. Why else are the nuclear powers holding on to their stockpiles? You think international treaties mean anything? We make a show of dismantling a few warheads, the other side does the same thing. Why, you ask? Because any man worth calling himself a man needs a trump card in case it hits the fan. Just for one thing, we, meaning America, can't feed or support our own, much less the rest of the world. We know that somebody has to go so the rest of us can live."

"You can skip the apocalypse routine. You're beginning to sound like a master-race theorist times ten."

McBain grunted. "It's no routine, nor any flight of the imagination, and there are certain people who should control the destiny of all men. It's already begun. It's all reached critical mass. Originally, yeah, I got on board for the money. But I was also a realist. I was a decorated hero in Korea, you know. I guess you could say my education in realism began back then."

"I have a file on you."

"But, of course. So did O'Malley. The Hydra file, right? I bet you have whatever he put together, but I'm sure it was nothing more than hunches on the senator's part, raising more questions than providing answers. He had numbered bank accounts, which was pretty much it. For all he really knew, they could have been CIA slush funds.''

"Is Hydra the name of an organization you've turned traitor for, or a code name for some strategy of destabilization and undermining or ruining of Third World countries?''

"The strong will inherit the earth, not the weak. A few strong and determined men can and will save the human race.''

"By, I assume, launching mass genocide?''

"It's what I've been leading up to. There is a plan to unleash war, famine, plague and pestilence on select, weaker countries who are sapping the strength of the ones who deserve to inherit the earth.''

"And, of course, you and your Russian comrades have put your heads together to save mankind.''

"Don't be so cynical of us, soldier. More than just Americans or Russians are involved. Our Coalition is nearly global. Anyway, what's the problem? It's always been about sabotage and subterfuge, assassination and anarchy—that's all the history of man has been about. War strengthens the naturally strong because the strong always prevail. And, in a comparable way, disease and famine are nature's way of eliminating those who would consume the strong. We are only here to speed up the process of nature. Then the strong roll in, pick up the pieces. To answer your question, yes, Hydra is the code name for our organization, which will save mankind and give its destiny a new face. We will use the ultimate forms of blackmail, and it won't just be nuclear. There are ways of mass death and destruction far worse than just being vaporized in a nuclear fireball.''

"Why tell me this?"

"Because you wanted to know. That's why I'm here. And because you can't stop us."

"How far does it reach, McBain?"

"Damn near around the world, I told you. Hell, it's been under way for almost twenty years. It all gelled when Russia went democratic and former foes became allies. When the old hard-liners were swept aside, what happened next? Chaos ruled Russia, and in steps the Russian Mafia. Crime, drugs, escalation of poverty, hunger, anger, widespread alcoholism and suicide—it's worse than ever in the motherland."

"You're saying the former KGB has decided to hold hands with the Russian Mafia to hurl Russia back into the days of Stalin."

"It's a little more complicated than that. Money talks, and, well, you know. But when the new world dawns, there will be no paper money, only bartering of human beings for the services, the talents or lack thereof they can provide. I'm not privy to all the details, but the current international trading system will become archaic."

"You've sold out to get rich and have homes around the world, McBain. How will you get along in a world without money? If the Russian Mafia knew it had no hope of monetary gain from your plan, why would it involve itself at all?"

McBain shrugged. "I'll still keep what I have by way of material possessions, and numbered bank accounts have proved more problems than they're worth. As for the Russian Mafia, if it doesn't want to stay on board, well, tough luck. They're nothing but thugs anyway. I assume tracking my money trail is how you've been able to figure out just how international we are."

Bolan ignored the inquiry. "It all sounds pretty insane to me."

"You're skeptical, but what you've seen so far, I think we've made something of a believer out of you."

"You've shown me you have to be stopped."

"How? Just you? And one other man, from what I've heard. Against an international army of soldiers, bankers, businessmen, politicians, intelligence agents, spies and superspies?"

"Whatever it takes."

Bolan's earpiece crackled with Grimaldi's voice. "Striker, another bad guy just stepped out of the vehicle. He's headed inside."

"Seems like your escort is about to join us," Bolan said.

"I'm sure he's come to take a look at the man who's caused us so much grief."

Moments later Bolan saw the tall man with bushy eyebrows open the stained-glass front door and step inside the café. The big figure he had seen from a distance in Cartagena wore a long black leather trench coat, beneath which Bolan suspected there was a weapon. The soldier braced himself for it to hit the fan. He waited while the tall man, watched by the proprietor and his patrons, closed on their booth. Bolan noted the scars on the man's face, then read in the dark eyes the look of a savage he had seen countless times before.

"No, I will not draw unnecessary attention to us at this time. I am Kuschka, whoever you are, the pain in our ass. You have had your time with the general. You have bit at our backs like an annoying insect for too long. I will be waiting up the mountain. I invite you to return soon, as I'm sure you intend to. General, it's time for us to leave."

True, the enemy had too much to lose and nothing to gain by starting a firefight in the village, Bolan knew. If official French law was drawn to the remote village, the enemy would have to fight its way out of the country. No matter how much money or influence the sinister organization wielded, it couldn't bribe an entire nation to do its bidding.

McBain rose, ground out his cigar in an ashtray, then put one last penetrating look on the soldier. ''Until we meet again.''

Silently Bolan watched as they left the café without another look back in his direction.

It was time to go back up the mountain.

9

"Apache to Striker, I'm going up. How are we looking on the rear and linkup time?"

Bolan headed the Land Rover into the mouth of a narrow gorge. From the town it was roughly a ten-mile run to the foothills. He had given the enemy a twenty-minute head start, then followed the dirt road leading from Beaumont Chalis to the gorge. Judging what he'd seen of the enemy so far—its money, manpower, resources and connections—Bolan figured either radar was tracking their movement or sentries were waiting in ambush. That the enemy knew they were coming and was ready wouldn't matter.

The coordinated ground-air strike was already worked out with Grimaldi, but it was going to be far from easy.

The sun had cleared the jagged eastern ridges. Blue sky above Bolan, with white clouds hovering over the distant snowcapped peaks. For the assault there would be no cover of darkness or relying on gullies or crevices in the mountainside for concealment. The two warriors fully expected to be met with every bit of firepower the enemy could throw their way.

Only Bolan's path would be paved with Grimaldi dropping the sky on the enemy from his Apache gunship.

"I'm one mile out and closing, Striker," Grimaldi answered the Executioner over his radio headset. "I'll fly over you. Anything shooting at you on the ridge, I'll take out first. There's nothing on your rear, no backup team from the town. So far, so good."

"I copy, Skywatcher. Hit them with everything you've got. Good luck. Over and out. See you after the fireworks."

It would be shaving it close until they linked up; even seconds could prove critical. According to satellite photos from Stony Man Farm, the trail leading to the château was about two hundred yards. Given what had happened during the night, Bolan expected armed sentries to start blazing away any second from the east and west ridgelines. He was out in the open, fully exposed to autofire or rocket fire.

Even still, the Land Rover's bodywork was lead plated, the windshield reinforced Plexiglas, but a steady barrage of autofire would eventually shatter the glass and a well-placed warhead would immobilize the vehicle. There was no other way, he knew, but a straight frontal charge at the enemy. Bolan had already shown them his hand—sniping them off, shaving down the odds. This time his trump card was minutes from being unleashed.

Beside Bolan the M-16 with attached M-203 grenade launcher was canted against the seat. His webbing was fitted with spare grenades for the M-203, fragmentation grenades and extra clips for the M-16, Beretta and .44 Magnum Desert Eagle.

He kept grim focus on the ridge and the rise. Tires bounced over the rocky terrain, the wheel fisted tight but shimmying in Bolan's hand as he gave the engine some gas. Climbing hard and fast, he scanned the jagged ridgelines on either side. So far, no waiting hard-force showed. The château stood roughly fifty yards beyond the rise. Bolan suspected they had ringed the perimeter with all available hands.

During the drive he had played back his face-to-face with McBain. If what the former general had told him was true, then a major international conspiracy between treasonous American military men and former KGB agents in collusion with the Russian Mafia was spinning some monstrous web of wholesale genocide. If the conspiracy was as well designed and ran as deep and as far as McBain claimed, then there was no telling who or how many were involved. There was a good chance government officials, either in Russia or America, were working behind the scenes to keep the enemy juggernaut rolling. Either way, Bolan knew the conspiracy didn't end with the enemy force in the Pyrenees. The enemy had a vision for a new world. It would come through bloodshed and anarchy, followed by oppression, domination and slavery. There were pieces still missing to the Hydra puzzle, but Bolan didn't intend to allow them to take one more innocent life.

The Executioner spotted the Apache AH-64 on his tail as it swooped into the gorge, the gunship's rotor wash kicking up a funnel of dust as it made its arrow-straight run for the rise.

No sooner was the gunship soaring over him than Bolan saw the enemy gunners show themselves on the ridgeline and cut loose with autofire.

CALHOUN'S HEART FILLED with murder. They were long overdue to nail the Colombians and get on with more serious business. What had happened in Colombia couldn't be changed; no amount of money could bring back the load or Calhoun's men, nor erase the shame and humiliation he felt. The Colombians were about to find out there was only one form of payment waiting for them here. Calhoun viewed the coming ambush as a moment of atonement.

The Colombians had arrived thirty minutes earlier, a crew of fourteen gunmen, and the one woman who turned out to be the daughter of the late Maldonado— a bastard child, most likely, who never made it into his file on the late drug lord. From what Calhoun could overhear, she was in charge, and her tirade, he imagined, boomed through the maze of halls and rooms of the château.

Disaster, either way, was coming for all of them. The Colombians could prove a fatal distraction. The problem that had dogged them to McBain's supposed safehouse and sniped off their men only a few hours ago was on the way back; it was the only logical course of action the unknown enemy would take. Now they were tied down dealing with the enraged Colombians, haggling over money, not to mention the woman demanding vengeance for her father's killing and making all manner of wild accusations.

Mini-Uzi wielded in his good hand, he listened to the woman railing about their loss, demanding immediate payment. Augustly, Morton, Commers and Teldren, armed with Ingram SMGs, trailed Calhoun down the winding stone steps that led from the upstairs bedroom. In sync with Kuschka's plan, they were moving in from behind, weapons up and ready. While the Russian offered conciliatory words, they crept closer to the targets. Of course, the Colombians were even angrier they had to wait for Kuschka and McBain to return from town.

Earlier Calhoun had gotten the word from Kuschka

and he had informed the Russian the Colombians had arrived. Arrangements were made over the radio: Calhoun was to make himself scarce, have Zholkovsky entertain. Calhoun wondered how the meet between McBain and their nemesis went, but this was no time for an update.

Calhoun fixed his gaze on the Colombians gathered in the dining hall, just beyond the archway. At the moment their backs stayed turned to him. His adrenaline surged.

The strategy was simple enough. Kuschka, McBain, the blond woman and six Spetsnaz commandos were sitting on the far end of the table. They would appear sympathetic, understanding of the Colombians while Calhoun and his four-man team slid into the dining hall, then opened up with their weapons while the Russians helped to nail the Colombians in a cross fire. A turkey shoot, hopefully, but Calhoun knew the Colombians would go down to the last man. Or woman.

Calhoun found the dark-haired woman with her back to him, an AK-47 slung across one shoulder. She was nearly screaming at Kuschka.

"We want our money. And the price has gone up for all the trouble you brought to us."

"I understand you are upset," Kuschka said, hands folded in front of him as he stood at the opposite end of the table.

"Upset! You sent your men to kill us at the warehouse in Marseilles."

"A misunderstanding. My apologies. I lost good men also. If we may speak frankly, I believe we have a common enemy. Two men. They are here in France."

"My father's organization is in near ruins! We have shipments that cannot go out now because of the attention, by way of your problems, that has been brought to us. We demand immediate payment for this disaster. And, yes, I have seen these two men. Twice they have killed my people and nearly myself! Convince me they do not work for you.''

Kuschka shrugged. ''Everyone must pay a price.''

''What are you saying? I asked you a question. We have much unfinished business!''

''Indeed, we do. I understand that life is tough.''

''What does that mean? The price is going up the more you stall!''

''Exactly what is it I am supposed to do for you? The kind of money you want takes time to get.''

''One call to your moneymen in Germany, and I'm sure the funds can be electronically transferred.''

Calhoun watched the woman, saw her gunmen, spread out down the table, standing guard. They were allowed to keep their weapons, a show of good faith on Kuschka's part. All eyes were focused on Kuschka as Calhoun led his men across the hallway.

Unfortunately the bulk of their combined force was stationed out in the courtyard. Still, Calhoun knew they could seize the moment by sudden lethal force and shock.

On each side of the gorge, along the ridge leading to the château, Kuschka had positioned two three-man fire teams. One team belonged to Kuschka, while the other was Calhoun's soldiers. From their vantage points they would be able to spot anything that moved on the château from all points of the compass. If the problem showed again, in broad daylight, Kuschka would be alerted and teams would move out to greet the bastard.

But first pick the irritant of the Colombians off their backs.

Calhoun was nearly at the doorway when one of the Colombians spotted him, his eyes widening in fear and shock.

"Maria! Behind you! It's a trap!"

The Colombians spun toward the doorway as a group. The Colombian who shouted the warning was bringing his AK-47 off his shoulder, barreling into the woman and knocking her to the floor, when Calhoun and his four-man team burst into the room, their weapons blazing, tracking and dropping a half-dozen Colombians where they stood.

From the other end of the table, Kuschka, McBain, Zholkovsky and the Spetsnaz commandos were already leaping to their feet. Pistols, subguns and AK-47s cut loose on the Colombians from the head of the table. Before they could react, the Colombians were locked in the cross fire of sizzling lead. They could do little else but scream in pain and rage, absorb bullets, dance jigs of death and topple. More bloody figures, chopped up by barking Makarovs or chattering subguns or Kalashnikovs, whirled in all directions.

Calhoun held back on the mini-Uzi's trigger, tracking on to Maldonado's daughter. She was rising, a snarl on her lips, her eyes burning with fury, when Calhoun stitched her across the chest, flinging her into the wall. Bullets snapped over Calhoun's head. He ducked, adjusted his aim, triggered a short burst into the chest of a Colombian in a white suit jacket. The onslaught of lead, tearing into the man from two directions, spun him on his heels before he pitched backward.

The din of weapons assaulting his senses, Calhoun saw his men spreading out, subguns stuttering on with lead messages of doom into several Colombians who held their ground, desperately trying to get off a shot.

They dropped on their backs, screaming obscenities, their weapons spitting harmless rounds into the ceiling.

It was over in a matter of a few seconds. Even McBain, Calhoun saw, was on his feet, a smoking mini-Uzi in hand.

When the last Colombian pitched to the table, Calhoun locked stares with Kuschka. For a moment, looking at the tall Russian through the smoky cordite, Calhoun saw the Makarov pistol in Kuschka's hand aimed his way. A strange look flickered through the Russian's narrowed gaze, then the Makarov dropped by his side. Calhoun didn't like the gesture at all. What the hell was that about? He sensed he was being judged right then. Perhaps even at some point in the future he would be considered more trouble than he was worth.

"They came a long way to get killed," Zholkovsky commented, all ice.

Calhoun looked away from the woman, found Sparrow moving for the radar terminal. "We've got movement, people, ground and air. Coming at us from the gorge!"

"He's here!" Calhoun said.

A moment later he heard the distant thunder of two explosions somewhere to the south. Kuschka was on his handheld radio, barking something in Russian.

"What the hell was that?" McBain asked.

"Our trouble has come with an attack helicopter," Kuschka announced.

McBain cursed. "After what happened to our ship, I would suggest, gentlemen, we pull in the troops and get the hell out of here unless we all want to be plastered up the mountainside."

"Move to the back of the building where the escape

tunnel is!'' Kuschka ordered, then grabbed his radio, barking orders in Russian.

Calhoun smelled the fear all around him, felt his heart pounding in his ears. A vision of the freighter being bombed by a fighter jet flashed through his mind.

Two HELLFIRE MISSILES got the full-frontal assault launched.

Bullets thudded off the lead-plated hood and roof, slashing across the Land Rover's windshield for all of two seconds before Grimaldi eliminated the threat of the fire teams on both sides of the ridge. Bolan kept the vehicle rolling uphill, didn't flinch when the missiles slammed into the ridgeline. The double blast rocked the ground beneath Bolan, and the sky above blossomed into a brilliant sheet of flames. Grimaldi flew on as bodies and rubble sailed away from the fireballs.

For the time being no more communication between the two warriors was necessary. If it moved, it was a target. Grimaldi's standing order was simple: pound the courtyard and front of the château, clear the way for Bolan to move in and cut them down. If at all possible he wanted a prisoner. Too many questions were still unanswered, and the soldier needed to know where the enemy's agenda led beyond France.

Bolan drove the vehicle into the rotor wash and swirling grit. Clearing the gorge on the final stretch, the soldier bounded the vehicle onto the plateau. He saw Grimaldi bank the Apache, level out and hover roughly fifty yards from the château.

The Executioner found the enemy on the courtyard grounds, weapons flaming away at the gunship, the bullets no more than beestings on the armored plating. A few of the gunmen, obviously knowing about the fighter jet that sank the drug ship, began to run for cover inside the château.

It was time to take the fight to the enemy, on foot, up close and personal. The relentless din of autofire rent the brisk mountain air as Bolan braked the vehicle to a jerky halt behind a large boulder.

Grimaldi went to grim work. At least a half-dozen Hellfire missiles streaked from the wings of the gunship.

Bolan hopped out of the vehicle, M-16 in hand. He gave the area behind him and his flanks a quick but hard search. There was nothing but smoking craters on the ridge.

The Apache began to lay down a blanket of total destruction on the courtyard. Bolan saw enemy gunners running for their lives through the front door. A missile struck the front of the building, hurling the runners inside on collapsing stone, wood and fire.

Bolan took cover from flying debris while Grimaldi hit them with another two Hellfire missiles. Vehicles were pulped to flaming ruins as the missiles struck dead-on. Bodies cartwheeled in all directions. Half of the front wall was reduced to piles of rubble. Fireballs hurtled twisted masses of metal into the front of the building. Mangled figures sailed in all directions, over the wall, off the plateau to plummet to a gorge on the other side.

Crouched, M-16 poised to fire, the M-203's breech loaded with a 40 mm grenade, Bolan moved out. Wreckage and bodies kept slamming the ground beyond the ruined front wall as the soldier quickly covered the short stretch of no-man's-land. A figure with an Uzi subgun staggered from the smoking maw of the front gate. He started to draw a bead on Bolan with his weapon, but the Executioner nailed him with a 3-round burst from his M-16.

Patching through to Grimaldi, Bolan said, "I'm going in."

Calhoun was hauling himself up from the rubble of the ballroom, choking on grit and smoke, when he heard Kuschka ordering, "Fall back!"

The ex-major shook his head, tasted the blood in his mouth. All around him men were pulling themselves from the stone, glass and wood shards that had come flying down the grand entrance hall on a series of deafening explosions. It seemed the west wall and the few standing marble pillars had buffeted them from ground zero.

Standing, grunting, Calhoun flexed his limbs, checking himself for serious injuries but finding nothing more than a few cuts and scratches. Not more than three feet ahead a slab from the stone ceiling and a toppled marble pillar lay in gouged ruins. One more second on the run before the sky fell, and he would have been crushed like an insect. Indeed, it had felt as if the whole mountain had collapsed on the château. He was beginning to wonder if the dead were the lucky ones, then shoved that defeatist thought out of his head. The body count out in the courtyard would be staggering. Even still, he found at least a full squad of combined Russian-American forces filing into the room. Some were covered in blood, others limping, most of them with a dazed look in their eyes. The wounded would have to carry themselves or be left behind. The standing order was suicide before capture.

Through the smoking holes in the front of the building, Calhoun found a few Russians and six of his own men running over the piles of debris. Outside there was nothing but flaming wreckage, strewed bodies. Suddenly a gas tank ignited from a twisted mass of metal, the orange fireball lighting up the inferno to a blinding dazzle. Calhoun flinched as a piece of wreckage razored from the blast, banged off the jagged teeth of the front wall.

Then he spotted the giant insectlike shape of an Apache gunship, hovering beyond the courtyard, roughly one hundred yards out. How could the enemy command that kind of firepower? One Hellfire missile alone, Calhoun knew, could take out a tank. In fact the gunship was known as a flying tank during the Gulf War. Several of their own pilots—if they were even still alive—had flown Apache tank killers against the Iraqis.

The mystery enemy, Calhoun seethed, had once again dealt them a crushing blow. But why not level the entire structure? Why hit the courtyard and just the front of the château? The enemy wanted a prisoner, he concluded. Logic dictated the gunship was covering for the bastard moving in on foot. Calhoun knew flight was wiser than fight at the moment. They were no match for Hellfire missiles. Once again, they had come up short.

"Now what?" McBain yelled, staggering to his feet.

"The tunnel, you said, leads to a cave that comes out the north side?" Kuschka bellowed.

Calhoun moved to join them, heard the stutter of autofire coming from the courtyard.

"Yes. Why?"

"We get to the airport and fly out of here," Kuschka answered.

"What about the enemy? Their gunship could blow us out of the sky," McBain argued.

"It's a private airport," Kuschka replied. "Whoever they are, I don't believe they will risk killing innocent civilians."

"What about when we're in the air?" McBain went on.

"It's a chance we'll have to take. My jets are certainly far faster than a helicopter."

"What about pilots?" Calhoun asked.

Kuschka nodded at three of his commandos. "They are right here."

Then Kuschka began giving the orders for three of his men to cover their retreat, before telling Calhoun to order three of his own to fall back, deeper into the hall. Calhoun gave the order to Tomlin, Cuttersworth and Jackley. Damn, he thought, searching the angry expressions of his men. He was losing soldiers fast, and by the minute, it seemed.

Calhoun was rooted to the marble floor for another long moment, listening to the autofire beyond. If they got out of the château without the missiles razing the place, if they got through the tunnel, to the airfield...

A lot of "if"s. Who the hell were those guys? he wondered. Undoubtedly they worked for some super-secret paramilitary organization, with or without the sanctioning of Uncle Sam, not that it mattered either way. The enemy was capable of tracking their every move even before they knew it, apparently, and hurling fighter jets and gunships at them. Calhoun gave the destruction around him another look. McBain had lost another private sanctuary. Calhoun knew the château had been a longtime safehouse for either McBain or some of his cronies in counterintelligence who had been on the run, selling secrets to the Russians.

Calhoun felt the warm stickiness running down the side of his face, wiped off the blood with the back of his hand. Pure luck was the only reason he was alive, Calhoun knew. How much longer would their luck hold?

"Major, what are you waiting for?"

Calhoun found Kuschka and the ice lady moving past the smoke and grit, disappearing into the narrow hallway for the back of the château. Calhoun moved out, almost wanted to apologize for leaving his men behind. Instinct warned him he wouldn't be seeing them at the airfield.

THE BLOODY WOUNDED staggered around the graveyard of flaming wreckage and mangled bodies. Bolan made the jagged teeth of the front gate, got busy dropping the enemy. He caressed the trigger of his M-16, kicking a gunman into the matchstick debris of a trellis near the far north end of the courtyard.

Return fire then slashed the inside of the wall, tracking on for Bolan. Through the drifting smoke and glowing band of fire, he pinpointed two crimson-soaked figures. One gunman was missing an arm at the shoulder, firing a French MAS assault rifle in a jerky sweeping motion. M-16 on full-auto, the Executioner flung both gunmen back into the flames of a demolished vehicle with an extended burst of 5.56 mm slugs.

Moments ago the soldier had observed maybe twelve to fifteen hardmen surging through one of three smoking holes in the front of the château. Cover behind the thick marble pillars had most likely saved them. Bolan glanced behind, looked up at the Apache.

He patched through to his air support and said, "Cover me. Once I'm inside, check the back. If it moves nail it."

"That's an affirmative, Striker."

On a zigzag run, the superheated crackle of flames drawing sweat from every pore, Bolan used the piles of rubble to make a quick advance on the demolished front of the building. He suspected a fair number of enemy gunners had survived. Their logical course of action was a fighting withdrawal. Further, they would most likely attempt to hike their way back down the mountain for the airport. It was at least a five-mile run for the airfield. Bolan and Grimaldi had already discussed a contingency plan if the enemy got that far. According to Stony Man Farm intelligence, it was a privately owned airfield used by tourists, European big shots who flew in to scale the Pyrenees or wander the countryside. He could be sure someone at the airfield had been well paid to maintain the enemy's aircraft and cover their flight plans. The enemy was using innocents to stabilize neutral turf, figuring their hunters wouldn't launch a massive strike on unsuspecting civilians and their property. Unfortunately for Bolan's purposes, they were right. Still, if his targets got that far and flew on, Bolan would track them down.

The moneymen were next on his shopping list.

Autofire rattled the air behind Bolan. Sizzling lead flying over the back of his neck, the soldier dived behind a pile of rubble from the front gate. Peering around the debris, he spotted two gunmen. The rage and pain on their faces looked demonic as they were lighted by intense fire. They surged from between fiery wreckage, holding back on the triggers of AK-47s. A moment later the two hardmen erupted into bloody sacks as Grimaldi nailed them with a thunderous barrage of 30 mm cannon fire.

Bolan headed forward, his eyes scanning his flanks. He was making his move on the middle gaping hole when a trio of gunmen cut loose with automatic weapons from that direction. Bullets slapped wreckage around Bolan as he charged at an overturned Jeep engulfed with flames. On the run, the soldier triggered his M-203. It was a hasty shot, and he could only hope he got lucky with a deadly score. The hell-bomb chugged away, but the enemy was already retreating deeper into the building. The grenade streaked through the opening, detonating somewhere deep inside the château. A muffled explosion sounded in the distance, followed up a short scream of pain.

Swiftly Bolan moved on, reaching the cover of a fallen pillar along the body-littered front steps. He stretched out in a prone position just as the gunmen swung back into the opening. Holding back on the triggers of their assault rifles, the two-man fire team hosed Bolan's cover. He hugged the ground behind the pillar while Grimaldi ripped into the opening with an extended barrage of cannon fire.

As soon as sharp cries of agony reached his ears, Bolan was up and running. He caught a glimpse of the savaged bodies falling backward, ejected the M-16's spent clip and cracked home a fresh magazine.

A glance over his shoulder revealed Grimaldi hovering over the courtyard. Flames, smoke and dust blew with gale force at the soldier before the ace pilot soared away to survey the back of the château. The soldier was clear from the courtyard to make his move for the enemy inside.

Bolan surged through the opening. Tracking autofire sounded from beyond the rubble piled in the grand entrance hall. Bullets drilled the wall behind him. On the fly, he counted at least three gunmen in the distance. Two were firing Uzi subguns from doorway entrances on either side of the hall. The other hardman blazed away with an Ingram from behind the splintered ruins of a large table.

Taking cover behind a pillar, Bolan loaded the breech of the M-203. Bullets stitched up the pillar, gouging stone. The soldier had no time for a standoff.

He took a frag grenade, pulled the pin and released the spoon. Crouched low, he whirled around the corner, hurling the steel egg.

"Grenade!"

Bolan bolted to the side as their weapons fell silent and they scrambled for cover. The grenade detonated in the middle of the hall, shredding the gunman behind the upturned table. As the hardman was hurled down the hall on the blast of fire and shrapnel, Bolan triggered the M-203.

The two surviving gunmen poked their heads around the corners of the doorways. Bolan figured they had to have glimpsed him in the open with the M-203 spitting out its grenade. They ducked back for cover. A curse ripped from beyond the swirling smoke and cordite as they disappeared inside each doorway a heartbeat before the 40 mm grenade punched into the wall. The explosion sheared off the wall concealing one gunman. Bolan heard nothing but the echo of the thunderous blast as he raced through the maze of rubble of the grand entrance hall. Finding nothing but strewed bodies, Bolan hugged the one standing wall. He heard coughing and gagging from inside the other doorway. A second later the gunman staggered from the opening. His weapon attempted to track Bolan, then his legs suddenly gave out and he pitched on his back.

Reaching the adjacent doorways, Bolan went in low to the room where the 40 mm grenade had struck. Inside he found several sprawled bodies. A quick check to make sure the dead were dead, then he heard a strangled cry of pain. Back in the hall, Bolan saw the remaining gunman reached for a side arm. The guy was lifting the Beretta's muzzle to his temple, but Bolan beat him to it, kicking the gun out of his hand.

Blood flowed from deep gashes on the enemy's head. Incredibly he was otherwise unscathed.

"Who...who the hell are you?"

"Your last hope at life," Bolan replied.

The soldier frisked the enemy, pulled a combat knife and tossed it down the hall.

"Where are the others?"

The enemy chuckled, then grimaced. "Gone. You're a little too late."

"You want to live?"

"Do I have a choice?"

"Yes. I take you from here, you talk and lead me to them, you've got a chance to see tomorrow."

He seemed to think about it, then nodded. "All right. It's...all blown up in our faces anyway. It's all too crazy to pull off. I'll help you."

"Smart choice."

Bolan patched through to Grimaldi. "Striker to Skywatcher, come in."

"Skywatcher here. No sign out back of the bad guys."

"I need you in here. We've got a live one willing to talk. Secure our prisoner while I take a look around."

IT WAS at least fifteen minutes after the prisoner was handcuffed when Bolan found the trapdoor in the far east end of the château. He stared down into the dark hole for a long moment, contemplating whether to follow the enemy. Finally he decided against giving chase. They had too much of a head start, plus Bolan knew he and Grimaldi needed to evacuate the mountain before the locals sounded the alarm. All right, their enemies would fly on, but Bolan would track them down no matter where they went.

The opposition would lead them to the next phase in dismantling the evil agenda.

Retracing his steps through the maze of back rooms, Bolan soon made it back to the ruins of the front of the château. He passed winding steps that led to the upstairs. At the far end of the hall, he saw Grimaldi, helmet in one hand, Uzi subgun in the other, standing guard over their prisoner.

Bolan strode on, then looked inside at the piled debris of what he recognized as the room on which he'd hit the enemy with a previous sniper attack. Beneath the shards of a table Bolan found the lifeless eyes of Maldonado's daughter staring back at him. If nothing else, he decided, a few loose ends had been tied up here. The last thing he and Grimaldi needed were vengeance-crazed Colombians throwing themselves into his hunt for the enemy.

The prisoner, who had told them his name was Jackley, was sitting against what remained of the wall where he'd taken cover. The man was bleeding from cuts on his head but otherwise he was unharmed, his shoulder-length black hair and mustache slick with crimson.

"Looks like your lucky day," Bolan said, reaching the prisoner. "The Colombians didn't fare so well."

"They got what they deserved. They came hunting for us, and we ambushed them."

"Us or them?" Grimaldi injected.

"Sort of like the underlying philosophy of the organization you work for, Jackley," Bolan said. "Where are the others going?"

Jackley hesitated, then stared up into the Executioner's steely gaze. "Munich. Since we lost the drug shipment, we need all available cash we can get our hands on."

"For what?" Bolan asked.

"The Coalition has been stockpiling component parts for nuclear reactors. A final shipment of enriched uranium and plutonium is set to be moved."

Jackley fell silent and Bolan growled, "I'm getting tired of having to lead you with questions. I want to know everything you know."

"You'll find the others in Munich, I swear. The Russians we work for helped to start an international bank called the World Bank Center. We need money for the next transaction, and they'll be running to Tielig and the moneymen in Munich."

"And this bank floats dirty money around the world for your organization, that much I know," Bolan said. "What I need is a bottom-line destination and goal. But tell me first, why join forces with a former KGB assassin? How deep does the money laundering go inside this World Bank Center?"

"Hard to say. There's front men, then I'm sure there's players in the background. Understand, at first this bank was supposed to help aid the fledgling democracy of Russia, with money, foreign investors. It was a smoke screen, of course. The bank is a main laundering center for money from the Russian Mafia. I'm not privy to all the details, but I know we've been funneling money from arms and drug transactions through it for at least a year. The president of the bank, Hermann Furst, was getting ten percent of our money to make sure the cash was delivered to Tielig's airport outside Munich. Tielig overextended himself, years ago, let others run his business while he blew money on pleasure. He doesn't even know whole planeloads of cash have been flying to the East, mostly to the Philippines.

"You want to know how deep this runs? Well, we've hired chemists, nuclear physicists who have been working around the clock on creating biological, chemical and nuclear weapons. They even bred, I've heard, a virus that can destroy food supplies, wheat, corn, like that. Understand, we're merely the frontline soldiers, tying up the loose ends of money and the gathering of a mercenary army from different countries."

"Like the terrorists Calhoun set loose on Manhattan?" Bolan said.

"It was a proving ground. The Russians wanted to see just how serious, loyal and determined we were. Kuschka and Calhoun go back for years, since Vietnam. Drugs and guns have always been their stock in trade. But then apparently, when Russia went democratic, Kuschka began forming his master plan with some of the old Communist hard-liners to return Russia to its days of iron-hand dictatorship."

"And you don't know exactly how this is all going to come about?" Bolan pressed.

Jackley shook his head. "I do know there's a plan to fly a cargo plane to Lebanon. A shipment of chemical weapons is to be delivered first to a group of Muslims who are going to pay Kuschka the money he needs to pick up the final shipment of uranium and plutonium in Pakistan."

Bolan paused and stared at Grimaldi, who said, "It looks like we've got our work cut out for us."

"You could have killed us all with that Apache," Jackley said. "I suspect you didn't in order to send the survivors running to the money source. I tell you what. If you make it to Germany, well, the Russian Mafia will be just about as unhappy as the Colombians over losing that dope. They'll be there."

"That's what I'm counting on," Bolan said, and hauled his prisoner to his feet.

He turned to Grimaldi. "You fly. I'll drive the two of us out of here and back to base."

The ace pilot nodded. "I'll have a jet fueled and ready to fly for Germany. What about touching base with our people to make arrangements for the next phase?"

"I'll handle that. Just get us to Tielig's airfield."

Grimaldi lifted an eyebrow, surprised.

"Right. I want the hornets out of the nest."

"How are we going to pull that off?"

"We'll play it like we're on the home team."

11

Above Germany

Only twenty-three of the joint Russian-American force had come down the mountain. Sitting in the front seat of the cabin of his private jet, Kuschka seethed over the loss of still more men and money, but choked it down in silence. He felt as if he had a time bomb in his belly. Worse, the only possible outlet for him to vent the murderous rage he felt was still alive and hunting for them.

Having already launched contingency plans over the long-range radio aboard the jet, the former KGB assassin stared out the cabin window at the sea of white clouds. They were twenty thousand feet in the air, the second jet with what remained of their forces from France flying to the starboard side. Moments ago the pilot had informed him they had crossed into German airspace. It wouldn't be long before they landed at Tielig's airfield.

Then what? Trouble was sure to follow. One fiasco after another was whittling down their force, the lightning attacks fraying their nerves, their hunters threatening to dismantle the whole operation. He even dreaded contacting his superiors in the Russian Far East to update them on the crisis they faced. He knew he couldn't postpone informing them indefinitely.

He thought about how they had been chased from the ruins of McBain's safehouse, scurrying through the tunnel like rats about to be drowned. It was shameful, running in the face of the enemy, but the nameless opposition had firepower that would have most certainly killed them all. How could two Americans inflict such incredible damage on them? Wherever they went, this unknown enemy appeared, hitting them with the kind of firepower that warned the ex-KGB assassin someone of authority in the U.S. government had sanctioned the two men to do whatever necessary to destroy them all. He couldn't help but wonder if Calhoun knew more than he was letting on. In time he would discover if Calhoun was holding out.

If another crisis threatened to derail their mission, then Kuschka might have to decide just how much he really needed the Americans. It certainly seemed as if all their trouble had begun with the terrorist attack in Manhattan. They had shown they could train and mobilize a fighting force, but Kuschka now had his own people to seek out, pay and mobilize more terrorist armies. He was becoming even more certain he didn't need the bloated baggage of McBain. The ex-general was long since out of the intelligence game. His contacts, namely the Colombians, had been used up. McBain was just along for the ride now, waiting to claim his own small country and vast fortunes and pleasure he had been promised. It was time, indeed, to reevaluate his need to keep the American allies on board. For the present, Kuschka decided to let them live. He would need the extra guns.

"It is time to strike back. The two Americans are sure to follow and find us in Munich."

Kuschka turned his head to look at Svetlana Zholkovsky. He had known her fifteen years, working with her on special assignments for the KGB. She was an accomplished assassin, trained in the martial arts and also a proficient sniper. Over the years he knew she had used her beauty and charm to get close to a male target where a man could not. He sensed his comrade and longtime lover had a plan.

Kuschka glanced over the seat. The cabin reeked of disinfectant and blood. Deep in the rear of the aircraft, the wounds of five soldiers were being cleaned and dressed by Kuschka's medic. Luckily their injuries didn't appear serious enough to keep them from firing a weapon.

He then found Calhoun and McBain, sitting side by side in brooding silence. Kuschka met their solemn eyes. Shortly he would have to address them all, inform them of the change of plans he had made yesterday in the event of disaster.

Kuschka returned his attention to the beautiful assassin from the Ukraine. They spoke in Russian. "What is it you suggest?"

"You have contacted Tielig, yes?"

Kuschka nodded. "The man is understandably angry and nervous. I told, or rather warned him, we need his continued cooperation and services. Cash is being loaded at a safehouse in the countryside near the Bavarian Alps. When we land, it will be ready to be transported and flown from his airfield."

"Only we do not go directly to Pakistan?"

"The final shipment of uranium and plutonium is being guarded by Colonel Turbat. The man is a notorious arms and drug dealer. He suspects he is being hunted by his own people. My contacts in Pakistan have confirmed this. He is anxious to fly out of Pakistan and join us, and he has gathered a small army of former Pakistani soldiers who will bolster our ranks. He has been paid, but only half. The last thing I need is another situation as we had with the Colombians. The Coalition is counting on us to return with the necessary men and matériel to begin the next phase. Lebanon is our next stop. We need money from the Shiites for the load of chemical weapons in order to pay Turbat.''

"I propose I go to see Tielig. I will stay by his side until our enemies show. I will make sure Furst gathers the remaining funds from our account. Tielig has become a liability. There is a chance he will talk to Interpol or even the American CIA. It was his ship that was sunk, after all. Questions are sure to come his way from the authorities.''

"Indeed. You will use yourself as bait to lure in our enemies?''

"Yes.''

"It is risky. Our enemies appear to strike at will, know our every move. But I know you. I have seen your work up close. If it were anyone else but you suggesting this...''

"I will pose as an associate of Tielig's.''

"Then what?''

"Kill them.''

"I would hate to see anything happen to you. Perhaps you are right. There is no other way than to attempt personal contact as a businesswoman, and then shoot them. I will send a backup team.''

"Fair enough.''

"We will be separated when you go to Tielig, but we will coordinate a linkup at Tielig's airfield.'' Kuschka rose, walked down the cabin. He searched their faces, finding anger and fear. "Comrades, there has been a change of plans. Major, you and your men will be flying on to Lebanon to stay with our Muslim friends, who are anxiously awaiting the shipment of chemical weapons. General, I will make arrangements for you to fly to the Philippines, where you will make ready your suite as a safehouse until I can contact our superiors and receive further orders. They might well arrive in the Philippines, awaiting my arrival with the Pakistan shipment. Arrangements have already been made for your transport. Are there any objections?''

Grim silence filled the cabin. Calhoun and McBain looked disgruntled and avoided Kuschka's penetrating stare.

"Do we have a choice?'' McBain growled.

"No, you do not. By the time we are reunited, the trouble that has followed us will have been dealt with.''

No one appeared brimming with confidence.

"That's it?'' Calhoun asked. "You scuttle us off in different directions, and we sit on our hands and wait for you?''

"No, that is not all. I will now give you a full briefing on how we are all to proceed. Understand, no more failures or setbacks will be tolerated, Comrades. I hope everyone is clear on what that means.''

"Death before dishonor,'' Calhoun said.

"Death before any further failure,'' Kuschka amended, and saw he commanded their undivided attention.

Siberia, Russia

ALEKSANDR NIKOLY watched from the window of his quarters as the Ilyushin transport plane touched down on the runway, misty funnels of snow spuming in the wake of the big bird's landing. He turned away, moved back for the bottle of vodka on his desk. He was no longer afraid, but rather was depressed that he would never leave this remote Siberian steppe to spend the cash in the suitcase by the table. It had all been for nothing. He had been used. It was only a couple of days ago, but he could still see the scarred face of Petre Kuschka out on the runway as if only minutes had passed. When Kuschka had flown off with the Spetsnaz commandos, leaving him utterly, miserably alone, instinct warned Nikoly he had fulfilled his purpose to the former KGB assassin.

Whoever was on the transport plane had come, he believed, to make certain the former gulag became his grave. He should have known better than to trust Kuschka, a man who enjoyed not only killing but causing others pain and suffering. Indeed, the ex-KGB assassin, he thought, was a devil in human skin. Kuschka had merely needed him for his former contacts in the GRU. An ex-colonel in the Soviet special forces, Spetsnaz, Nikoly had found the former commandos in and around Moscow to be handed over as, he suspected, cannon fodder for whatever devious plan Kuschka had in mind.

Nikoly poured himself a vodka, waiting. Long minutes passed, giving him time to think about the wrong turn he had made. It was pointless, he decided, to brood about his life. Greed had simply gotten the best of him.

There was a knock on the door. "It's open."

Nikoly watched as the door opened and two men slowly entered the Spartanly furnished quarters. They had the same cold, dead eyes he had seen on Kuschka.

They wore long black coats, and the bulge of a holstered pistol was visible near each man's shoulder.

Nikoly shivered against the bitter cold that howled through the doorway. The taller of the two men said, "Aleksandr Nikoly?"

"You know who I am. Would you come in and shut the door."

The shorter one grunted, looking at Nikoly with disdain. Nikoly drank what he suspected would be his last drink as they entered the room and shut the door.

"Is the money in that suitcase?" the tall one asked.

"I believe that is what you came for."

"Our plans have changed."

"You mean Kuschka's ordered you to safely escort me out of this frozen wasteland?" Nikoly said, then chuckled bitterly.

"You knew it had to end this way," the tall one said, reaching inside his coat and pulling out a Makarov pistol.

"What I know is that I had a deal with Kuschka to produce the necessary former Spetsnaz troops for a large sum of money. What I don't understand is why did you leave me here to rot in fear, waiting for your return to execute me? Why give me any hope? Why leave the money?"

"We needed to know if you were followed by anyone from Moscow," the short one replied. "We have had the compound under aerial surveillance."

"Funny, I have heard no aircraft fly over the past two days."

"You may have, had you not been busy swilling vodka," the tall one said.

Nikoly turned angry. "I don't know how you plan to pull if off, but Kuschka and the old-line guard from the

KGB and military he works for are insane. What is it? Nuclear blackmail? Storm the gates of the Kremlin and throw Russia back into the dark ages of Stalinism?''

"I am privy to few details," the tall one said, holding his pistol low by his side, "but I do know a major revolution is slated for Russia. The entire world will tremble soon, from what little I know of the plans of my superiors. We will have the necessary weapons by then to hold hostage any smaller nation of our choosing, and more specifically, these new republics in our motherland."

Nikoly killed his vodka. "You are as mad as the others. I caught rumblings from former contacts in Moscow, weeks ago, that something horrific was being planned. Perhaps I was fed information to draw me out, test my loyalty to Kuschka."

"In our country, you, having worked intelligence with the GRU, know that anything is possible."

"I am glad I will not be here to see the horror and madness you propose to unleash. You do not answer my questions very well. I feel it is the least you could do. Call it a last request."

"What is it you wish to know?" the short one asked.

"How many are involved in this conspiracy?"

"Many. Far more than you could guess. Answering your questions does not matter."

"I can see how things in our country have come to this. We have rampant crime, food shortages, unemployment. With democracy came the ills of the West. But it is always like this in Russia. We live for chaos, even destruction, in order to rebuild ourselves. Strangely enough I am not bitter that Kuschka has betrayed me. I tell you, this madness you seek will not happen."

"How can you be so sure?" the tall one asked.

"I know there is a counterintelligence, counterrevolutionary organization in our country that watches for just this sort of thing. Perhaps they have contacted the American CIA for assistance. What I'm saying is that someone most likely knows by now of your plans. Someone will come hunting for you and crush you before this madness happens. There are no secrets in our country."

The short one grunted. "Who is going to stop us?"

Nikoly shrugged. "I don't know. But I have been around long enough, seen enough to know that there is always someone around who is smarter, tougher, better. I have been outsmarted, bettered by Kuschka, but his day will come."

They exchanged dark looks, then the tall one said, "Do you wish to do it or do I?"

Taking the bottle, Nikoly filled his glass, then killed the vodka. He looked his assassin straight in the eye and said, "You may have the honors."

12

Munich, Germany

She watched Max Tielig squirm in his wing-back chair, disgusted by his lack of nerve and resolve to deal with the present crisis. She crossed her black-nyloned legs, studied the German import-export entrepreneur for several moments.

He sat behind his massive white-marble desk. The German's suite was more a testament to pleasure than business: stereo and giant-screen television built into the oak walls; wet bar, whirlpool, a long white sofa, glass coffee table and a short table with six chairs on either side, used for a rare business conference, she suspected. Outside, in the main lobby, a skeleton work force, including two secretaries and a receptionist, milled around or sat in cubicles, monitoring computer banks.

"This whole business with you people has cost me dearly!"

Impatient, tightening her jaw, she listened to him rail, waiting for him to vent his outrage. The Russian Mafia, working with Kuschka, had been doing business with Tielig or the man's subordinates for some time. But this was her first meeting with the man; it would also be her last. The sight of him, near hysterics, worrying only about his own problems, was making her seethe. The

German had no neck, was built like a fire hydrant. He was short and squat, and his silk suit looked ready to burst from the excesses of soft living. It didn't escape Svetlana Zholkovsky that his eyes would wander over her long shapely legs or glance at her breasts straining against the sheer white silk of her blouse.

She wanted to look the role of a businesswoman, having just bought the outfit on the drive into Munich from Tielig's airfield. She wore a black suit jacket, matching skirt with a kick pleat and high heels. A leather briefcase beside her chair put the finishing touches on what she hoped would be a ruse sufficient to get her targets to drop their guard. She had the briefcase open, some blank papers inside for show, a handheld radio to contact her backup team that was parked and waiting in the underground garage. The Makarov pistol was also in the briefcase, a 9 mm round chambered. She suspected if their enemies were going to contact Tielig or simply show up, it would be soon.

"I have lost millions of dollars, not to mention a ship. Not to mention the crew I hired who have families I have to answer to."

"They were hired guns, Max. Calm down. Very few of them had wives and children. Nearly all of them had long criminal records or were simply mercenaries interested only in money. They knew the risks going in."

"Indeed. A fighter jet blows up my ship! Tons of cocaine floating around the Caribbean! Do you not think the authorities, Interpol, the American Justice Department, the DEA, maybe even the CIA will want to question me? Not only that, now I am being shadowed by thugs from the Russian Mafia."

She looked at the black box on the desk, asked, "What is that?"

"It brings up the slats against the windows."

She took the box. Looking past Tielig, she gazed at onion-shaped domes of a church. To her the twin towers of the cathedral looked like beer mugs. She punched a button on the box, looking away from the Munich skyline. A soft whir sounded, then white marble slabs rose. Tielig stood as shadows fell over the suite. He was grumbling something in German as he went to the bar, flicked a switch on the wall. Soft white light shone from the ceiling. She watched him build a drink.

"Not offering me one, Max?"

"Would you care for a drink?"

"Sit down, Max."

"And do what?"

"Wait."

"For who?"

"The ones who sank your ship."

He moved back to the desk and plopped into his chair. He rubbed his face, sighing, drinking.

Smiling, enjoying his fear, she felt the leather sheath with its stiletto inside, snug against her thigh. When the targets were eliminated, she would then take care of Tielig, rejoin Kuschka and the others at the airfield.

"How do you know they will come here? And who are they?"

"They will be here. It is their next logical step. They know something about the money behind our operation. That would involve you, and it would others, namely Hermann Furst."

"The World Bank Center is a reputable international bank."

"Run by crooks. Please. We all know what is going on here. And I am here to conclude urgent business, and you will not leave my sight until it is finished. Further, who they are is not important. You only need to know they pose a great danger to all of us. If we fall, you fall, Max."

"Kuschka sent you. So what's he doing while you baby-sit me?"

"Taking care of business with Furst. I urge you to remain calm and do exactly as I tell you. You follow my lead. I assure you, despite your piggish thinking, one mere woman can and will dispose of our enemies."

"I did not ever think I would see this sort of trouble, but I should have known better than to deal with ex-KGB and Russian Mafia. This is a nightmare."

"Max, you weren't thinking of leaving Munich and leaving us to face all these problems alone, were you?" She read the lie in his hesitation even before he answered.

"Of course not. How can I go anywhere with the Russian Mafia all over this city?"

"They want their shipment."

"So, what are you going to do? A round-trip ticket to Colombia, hand them some scuba gear?"

"I do not think this is a time for jokes."

"Who's joking? I'm trapped here."

"You have security?"

"They pick me up when I leave."

"I'm your security detail now, but we'll make arrangements to give your people some time off in a while."

Tielig turned grim. "What about these men you say will be coming here? What will you do? Kill them right here?"

She smiled, said nothing.

"THIS IS an unauthorized landing! Who are you people?"

Bolan walked away from the Learjet, pinning the lean, balding man with an icy stare.

The Executioner fell into his role as an associate of his enemies. "The major, the general and Comrade Kuschka are expecting us. I'll ask the questions. What's your name?"

The German balked, then squared his shoulders. "Gortslip. I am in charge of this airport. I have been told nothing by any of the three men you mentioned that you would be arriving."

Behind Bolan, Grimaldi led their prisoner away from the jet. Jackley was uncuffed at the moment, but the ace pilot had the cuffs in a pocket of his coat, ready to snap them on their prisoner when they were clear of the airport. Once they were airborne from their temporary base near the Pyrenees, Jackley had cleaned his head wounds under Bolan's supervision. Some stitching by the soldier, and the bleeding had stopped. It all looked suspicious, but Bolan felt he had no other option than to bluff his way through Gortslip while Grimaldi kept Jackley close at hand.

The two warriors carried duffel bags large enough to hold grenades, their Uzi subguns, spare clips for the SMGs and side arms, their webbing and other gear necessary to resume the hunt. Beneath his coat, Bolan carried the Beretta and the .44 Magnum Desert Eagle. Their M-16/M-203 over-and-under combos were locked in a bin inside the jet.

Bolan looked around the airport. Twin-engine planes, private jets and executive helicopters were parked near hangars. Two cargo planes stood at the far north end of the airfield. No aircraft was flying in or out at the moment. There was no sign of the enemy's private jets, but Bolan figured they were grounded in a hangar. An office in the distance and a control tower completed the picture of a business mogul's private airport. Bolan couldn't discount the fact his enemies could be watching from the office building, but he believed they were already en route for Munich or rounding up money from one of their legitimate brokers.

Bolan looked at the white van that had rolled up to greet them when Grimaldi landed. It was parked on the runway, beyond the bald German. Two men in white coveralls stood beside the vehicle. If they had come with weapons, then they were inside the van. It looked as if transportation would be provided, courtesy of Gortslip.

During the flight Bolan had radioed Brognola. The Learjet was complete with fax machine, radio console and computer linkup to Stony Man Farm. Once the big Fed was up to speed, he had faxed maps of Munich with detailed routes to the homes and businesses of the moneymen on the soldier's hit list. While the two warriors took the fight to their enemies in Munich, Brognola would lay the groundwork for the next leg of the mission. Of course, Bolan knew getting to Lebanon for the next phase all depended on what happened in Germany.

"I believe I should contact the major or the general about this," Gortslip said.

"Do that and I will inform them just how uncooperative you've been. Their business here is urgent, requires the utmost discretion. I can assure you they will take great offense to being disturbed by any contact from you about me."

The German scowled. "I don't like this."

"You don't have to like it. I will need that van," Bolan said. "I also want this jet fueled and ready to fly when I return here with my comrades. Do not touch or inspect anything inside or you will answer to me personally. Am I making myself clear, Gortslip?"

"This is all highly unorthodox."

"Answer my question."

"Very well. I do this with great reluctance...."

"I don't care how you do it."

Bolan looked over his shoulder and told Grimaldi, "Let's go."

Feeling the German's suspicious eyes boring into the back of his head, Bolan slid open the side door of the van. Grimaldi held the door for the prisoner as Bolan kept an eye on Jackley, who got in on the front passenger's side. Moments later Grimaldi took over the driving duties and fired up the engine.

As they rolled away from the trio of Germans, Grimaldi said, "That might have been the easiest part. If he makes a call, we could find the whole crew of bad guys waiting for us when we get to Tielig's office.

Bolan unzipped his duffel bag and pulled out a cellular phone. He took a computer printout, then glanced at the number to Tielig's office in downtown Munich.

Grimaldi caught his friend's eye in the rearview mirror. "Is that what we're counting on?"

"Rats in a barrel."

"Just lay it out how you want me to proceed."

If what their prisoner said was true, then the enemy had come to Munich to tie up the loose ends on money matters, or extort their front men for more money. However the numbers fell, Bolan knew Munich would be jammed with innocents. Visions of how casually the enemy had used human shields before flashed into Bolan's memory.

He heard a woman's voice answer on the other end and said, "I need to speak with Herr Tielig."

She wanted him to identify himself, but Bolan simply told her Tielig was expecting his call. He was told to wait a minute, then a rough voice on the other end said, "Tielig here. Who is this?"

"Your problem from overseas. Listen up, this is what I want you to do."

IT WAS TIME to reach out and touch the German business mogul.

Bolan had ordered Tielig to give his employees the day off, told him to be waiting in his office alone. Tielig was as dirty and savage as the men he fronted for. He didn't pull the trigger on a weapon, but he aided their operation, giving them transport, providing them contacts and services in the World Bank Center, helping them to channel illicit funds into shell companies. After some interrogation to get a clear fix on the enemy's current movements and plans, Bolan intended to use Tielig as walking bait to reel the enemy in.

As ordered by Tielig through Bolan, the parking attendant had allowed them to roll past the gate and into the underground garage without a ticket or any hesitation. Tielig's suite was on the top floor. According to Stony Man Farm, the building was owned by the World Bank Center. Built two years ago, it was the nerve center of varied businesses that were bankrolled by the WBC. They ranged from a computer hardware outfit, a travel agency, to the brokering of gold and diamonds down to an accounting firm. Behind the facade of legitimate business, Bolan knew other endeavors such as arranging the smuggling of contraband, were working overtime.

Grimaldi drove deep into the belly of the garage, winding the van around a ramp to the bottom level. Bolan looked over his shoulder.

"I didn't see anything that looked like a tail on the way in," Grimaldi said.

Bolan fixed the sound suppressor to his Beretta. He took out his handheld radio. "I'll leave it on. If there's trouble..."

"I'll be there."

"Cuff our friend after you park."

Grimaldi found a slot at the deepest end of the garage. He backed the van in, killed the engine, then snapped the cuffs on Jackley.

"What are you going to do?" Jackley asked Bolan. "Start killing legitimate businessmen?"

"Tielig's helped you people get around. By boat and plane. He was in on that drug deal. Indirectly he helped kill a lot of people, most bad, but some good."

"I'm thinking, Striker," Grimaldi said, "if it goes south, well, being stuck in this garage and having to face the German police may be the start of a major headache for us."

"I hope to keep it simple. This is a roundup. I'll give Tielig the only option available. Play ball or he's out of the game. Either way, be ready for anything."

Bolan scoured the garage. At the moment they were alone, but nearly all the parking spaces were full. It was too still, too quiet at that hour for Bolan's liking. Combat instincts were flaring. He had a feeling they were being watched, but couldn't pinpoint any shadows or occupants in vehicles.

Of course, he had no idea what he would find upstairs. He didn't think the enemy would be lying in ambush in a public building. They had too much to lose to get embroiled in a gun battle with the German police. Still Bolan and Grimaldi had them on the run, scared and desperate.

The Executioner got out. Swiftly he moved for the service door that would lead to the lobby.

13

Bolan took the service stairs to the top floor. If the enemy was waiting, then riding the elevator would provide all the edge necessary to trap him, cut him down as soon as the doors opened. Still the soldier was gambling neither the enemy nor Tielig wanted to draw unnecessary attention to themselves with an all-out firefight in a secure public building.

Just in case he was wrong, the Executioner carried three frag grenades in the pockets of his coat. In the event the enemy was massed in large numbers, a fighting withdrawal would be in order. At some point they would have to leave the building. Bolan needed either Tielig or his enemies to lead him to wherever they were making ready for their Lebanon departure.

The silenced Beretta 93-R set on 3-round-burst mode, Bolan turned the door handle. Crouched, he opened the door a few inches, peered beyond, combat senses on full alert. The hall led past the elevator bank to a glass partition beyond, which was the reception area. The outer office of the massive suite appeared empty at first surveillance. Bolan listened to the silence. Lights were flashing over the two elevators, indicating workers in the building were getting on or off on the lower floors.

Bolan raised his handheld radio. "I'm in."

Grimaldi answered back, "Nothing down here other than a few employees heading out."

"Watch yourself down there. There should be more activity by way of employees going in and out. It's lunch hour."

"I'm watching your back. If I see something, you'll be the first to know."

And hopefully not the last, Bolan thought. He went back years, countless hellfire missions with Grimaldi. They had come this far and inflicted serious damage on the enemy. Grimaldi was a good friend, the best damn pilot Bolan had ever known and a true warrior. The man would go the extra mile for Bolan, had put his life on the line time and again, against the savages who would devour the innocent in the name of greed, blood lust and domination. Bolan had known and fought alongside Grimaldi for so long, the memories of when they had been adversaries seemed like a distant and forgotten bad dream.

Bolan left the handheld radio on, moved into the hall and swiftly skirted the elevator bank. He opened the glass door to the reception area. The work bays and cubicles were empty, computer screens blank. It appeared Tielig had given his staff the day off as ordered, canceled any appointments.

Bolan gave the outer office a final search. Something felt wrong. He found Tielig's name engraved on gold plate on a set of double doors. The silence beyond the doors disturbed the soldier.

He knocked on the door, staying in a crouch. He wasn't being overly paranoid thinking bullets could start drilling the door from beyond. "Tielig?"

"Yes. Come in!"

"Come here and open the door."

If it was a trap, the German businessman would be the first one to go.

"What?"

"Do it. Now."

Bolan waited. Moments later the door opened. Shock bulged Tielig's eyes as the Beretta was thrust in his face. Spinning the German, Bolan marched him into the suite. Then the Executioner saw the blond woman, a look of fear in her eyes as she rose from her chair in front of the desk. She had some papers in her hands. Beyond her shock and fear, Bolan thought he detected something else. But what? Was she measuring him? Remembering something? Or had the moment simply put him on edge?

"What is the meaning of this? Who are you?" she cried.

Bolan scoured the suite. There appeared no other ways into the suite, but he maintained vigilance, braced for the unexpected.

"I thought I told you I wanted us to be alone," the soldier growled.

"I am Savrina Dorchovsky, whoever you are. I was in an important meeting with Herr Tielig when you barged in here. I demand an explanation before I call security."

The plan was shot. Bolan could be identified by the woman. He decided he would have to tie her up, evacuate, hope for the best, which meant eluding the German authorities long enough to catch up to Calhoun and the others.

"Who is she?" Bolan growled in Tielig's ear, shoving the German away.

"A close business associate. We were just concluding business."

Tielig was stumbling on rubbery legs toward his marble desk.

Bolan looked at the woman. She had a thick accent, Eastern European, or perhaps Russian. He told the woman, "It's concluded."

"Well, in that case, I will be on my way."

"You're staying, and you'll do exactly what I tell you," Bolan said.

She stared at Bolan for a long moment, then icy coldness fell over her face. Instinct warned Bolan something about the woman wasn't what it seemed. Long strides carried him to the desk.

"Stay put, Tielig," he ordered. Bolan noted there was no view of the Munich skyline. He wondered why the windows had been partitioned off with the marble slabs, the sunlight shut out. It was beginning to feel more wrong with each passing second.

"If you will allow me to put these papers away...and I need a cigarette. You are scaring me. Who is this man, Max?"

Bolan stood beside the desk on the far end from Tielig and the woman when he saw her reaching into her briefcase. She was suddenly too calm and deliberate. There was a subtle change in her expression and voice that set off an alarm in Bolan's head.

The soldier discovered the reason for the mood swing a second later.

The Makarov leaped out of her briefcase like a cobra striking from the brush.

Tielig cursed, hit the floor.

Caught off guard, knowing he could never adjust his aim in time to shoot her, Bolan dived behind the desk as the Makarov fired a single 9 mm round.

"YOU TWO HAVE GOTTEN pretty lucky so far. Who do you work for? You're too good to be CIA, unless you're part of some black-ops team."

Grimaldi watched the garage in both directions. They were alone. Jackley had his hands cuffed in front of him. Grimaldi felt the man's stare boring into the side of his head. He reminded Grimaldi of a frightened cornered animal. Now the guy wanted conversation, either just to hear himself talk or calm his nerves.

"You wouldn't believe me if I told you," Grimaldi said.

He was worried about Bolan, going up alone. With the radio on he continued to monitor the Executioner's movements, then heard the sudden angry exchange when Bolan discovered he wasn't alone with Tielig. Grimaldi's heart raced. He was torn between staying where he was or putting the prisoner out with a crack over the head with his Llama autopistol and going up to the suite when another situation drew his attention.

Grimaldi spotted the three big men in black leather trench coats at the far end of the garage, beside the service entrance. One by one they leaped over the concrete railing from the next level up, landing with catlike grace. They didn't even bother to look his way or even give the lower level a glance. They didn't look like German police or a security detail for the building. A moment later one of them confirmed Grimaldi's worst suspicions. The gunmetal of a Stechkin machine pistol showed as the man threaded a sound suppressor to the muzzle.

Trouble.

Grimaldi was reaching for the handheld radio to alert his friend when all hell broke loose. First Grimaldi heard the cracking report of a pistol over the radio.

Then, as he was looking toward the prisoner, the cuffed double fists slammed him in the jaw. Lights erupted in the ace pilot's eyes as his head bounced off the driver's window. If the prisoner had a little more leverage behind the twin punch, Grimaldi knew he'd be out cold.

Then he felt hands clawing inside his coat, heard the prisoner snarling like a mad dog in his ear. Adrenaline and grim determination cleared the cobwebs long enough for Grimaldi to grab Jackley's hands.

But the Llama autopistol was out, and Grimaldi found the weapon locked in both their hands. Suddenly the gun shook in their viselike grips as it boomed a round near Grimaldi's ear. Deafened by the thunder of the shot, the Stony Man pilot thrust the prisoner's hands up as another round cannoned into the ceiling. He felt the prisoner's fury, heard the growling break through the ringing in his ears. Grimaldi saw the bared teeth, inches from his eyes, Jackley's eyes wide and burning with savage determination. Banging his foot back into the driver's door, the pilot threw everything he had into propelling himself forward. Somehow he managed enough leverage to hurtle Jackley across the van.

Only Jackley clutched the gun, fisted a handful of Grimaldi's jacket and took the pilot with him. The two men hit the other door, the force of their combat driving Jackley's head through the window in an explosion of glass.

Still Jackley held on to the gun, snarled and strained to bring the autopistol down from the ceiling. Grimaldi reared his arm back, fist balled to pulp the prisoner's nose with one crushing blow, when a knee speared into his groin. The excruciating pain blinded the pilot for an eternal few seconds. He almost lost his hold on the autopistol, then felt Jackley shove him with near superhuman strength, forcing Grimaldi to his back on the floorboard behind the front seats. A grunt of pain reached Grimaldi's ears as he realized he pulled the enemy with him.

The Stony Man pilot looked up at the face of hate and rage. He slashed a right off Jackley's jaw, but the man was consumed with murderous intent. With Jackley's weight on top of him, Grimaldi knew the man had the leverage to eventually force the autopistol down, aim it at his face or chest. The pilot had one chance. He kept one hand locked on the gun as he slid a leg up, reached into the ankle sheath and drew his combat knife.

Jackley forced the pistol toward the side of Grimaldi's head. The hardman's finger curled around the trigger as he drove the barrel closer to Grimaldi's face.

In one smooth motion the ace pilot speared the blade deep into his adversary's neck, then wrenched it across Jackley's throat. With a look of horror etched on his face, the hardman dropped the Llama autopistol, clutching at his slashed throat.

As soon as he made the killing slash, Grimaldi kicked Jackley in the chest, avoiding the torrent of blood as he rolled into the side door.

The pilot stared into Jackley's bulging eyes. The life fading in his stare, his hands still grabbing at the gaping yawn across his throat, Jackley toppled forward.

Grimaldi scanned the garage. Fortunately he was alone, but with a dead man. He searched for the handheld radio. An ambush was heading Bolan's way, but from the sound of gunfire coming over the radio, he suspected the Executioner was already in serious trouble.

THE BULLET MISSED Bolan by a fraction of an inch. Another slug whined off the desktop as the soldier took cover behind the desk, scurried for the far end. It had been a trap all along. The ruse of a businesswoman, shocked by the sight of a stranger with a gun, had nearly worked. But Bolan had seen enough treachery and deceit over the years to trust his instincts when something felt wrong.

He had one shot, less than an eye blink to act.

He got lucky in the next instant.

Popping up, he glimpsed the woman stepping forward, her Makarov aimed at the other end of the desk where Bolan had been a heartbeat earlier. She adjusted her aim, but Tielig panicked, bolted to his feet and staggered into her line of fire.

Bolan caressed the Beretta's trigger, taking advantage of the only edge he would get. A look of anger and surprise hit the woman's face as she realized Tielig had unwittingly given her adversary a fatal edge. A trio of 9 mm slugs coughed from the Beretta, drilling ragged crimson holes across her chest, shredding white fabric. The triple impact carried her back in a stumbling dance. Still grasping the Makarov, she pitched backward, crashing into the glass coffee table. Among the jagged shards, she twitched once, then lay utterly still.

Bolan charged after Tielig, shouting, "Stop or I'll shoot."

Tielig halted in midstride several feet from the door. He lifted trembling hands above his head.

"Striker! Striker, come in."

Bolan pulled out the handheld radio. "It was a trap. I've got Tielig and I'm coming down."

"You've got trouble headed your way. Three goons, looked armed with machine pistols with suppressors.

They entered the service entrance maybe two minutes ago. Jackley's dead.''

"What happened?"

"He came at me like a demon, went for my gun. It's a mess in here."

"Do you have a vehicle in the garage?" Bolan asked Tielig, knowing they had to abandon the van. Even still, it was a long shot to elude the German authorities once someone discovered the dead female assassin in Tielig's suite. And it looked as if the body count would pile up even more. So far, their luck had held up. No confrontation with official law. That could change anytime, and it would take all the clout Brognola could muster to free them from the German police. Bolan wouldn't gun down a lawman, no matter what. Right then he had more pressing matters to deal with.

"Yes. Well, I had a three-man security team."

"Where?"

"They're gone. The woman ordered me to give them the day off. I have my own private vehicle below."

"Keys?"

"In my pocket."

"Sit tight," Bolan told Grimaldi. "We'll take Tielig's vehicle. I'm on my way."

Rolling over Tielig and grabbing the German by the shoulder, Bolan asked, "Who was she?"

"An assassin. Sent here by Kuschka to kill you."

"And she had backup?"

"I believe."

"Well, they're on their way. Try to run, and I won't hesitate to shoot you. I'm your only way out of this building alive."

Bolan shoved Tielig out of the office. Two minutes, more or less, he thought. If they took the service stairs, it would mean a five-minute hike, at least. Out in the hallway Bolan saw the light on the elevator flashing from one floor to the next. He backed up, waiting. He forced Tielig to his knees.

The light above the door flashed on eleven.

Bolan gripped the Beretta with both hands.

Twelve.

He sucked in a breath, then exhaled.

The doors slid apart, and three big men were bringing silenced Stechkin machine pistols from beneath their coats, realizing the danger too late, when Bolan cut loose with the Beretta. Anger hardened their faces, then shock formed their death masks as the Executioner swept the trio, left to right. The silenced Beretta chugged out 3-round bursts, blasting apart their chests. One machine pistol stuttered brief but aimless return fire. Tielig cried out in alarm as the goon's rounds drilled marble above his head. They spun, hit the sides of the glass-walled elevator. Momentum sent them crashing into glass. Blood sprayed their reflections a millisecond before the force of their hammering weight cracked the mirrors into a giant spiderweb.

Bolan grabbed an ashtray stand beside the elevator. The doors closed, but he used the ashtray to keep them wedged open. Hopefully the floors were thick enough to provide a sound barrier to the racket of the lethal engagement. Soon enough someone below would notice the elevator was stuck on the top floor.

By then Bolan hoped to have evacuated the garage.

He tugged Tielig toward the service stairs.

The enemy was desperate enough to strike at them anyplace, anytime, from out of nowhere, not giving a damn about the consequences, unmindful of innocents or confronting the police.

Either way, Bolan knew they were in a race against time, catching up to the enemy while staying clear of the German authorities.

14

Kuschka led his team into the massive conference room. It had been a long and nerve-racking drive down the Autobahn from Munich. Kuschka had placed the calls, had, of course, been forced to make the necessary threats to gather the key moneymen at a moment's notice. Even still he had been assured the money would be in the chalet that was nestled in the foothills of the Bavarian Alps. Naturally he was suspicious, even paranoid of what he might find at the chalet.

The Russian had been here twice in the past, both for pleasure in the form of vodka and prostitutes, and to conduct business with the president of the World Bank Center. This day the conclusion of their business was a matter of life or death.

The three Germans who were the driving force behind the World Bank Center watched with mixed reactions as the Russians rolled in, armed to the teeth. His trench coat open to display the Stechkin machine pistol slung across his shoulder, Kuschka stood at the head of the black marble table. Beneath the soft yellow overhead lights, their faces looked somber. Finally Kuschka looked at Hermann Furst. The stocky, dark-haired president of the WBC was scowling around the room at the show of force.

Kuschka had linked up with six members of the Rus-

sian Mafia in Munich to bolster his twelve-man Spetsnaz team. His comrades in the Russian Mafia were understandably angry thcy had lost their share of the drug
shipment. Kuschka had offered compensation to the
Dmitrov brothers, Ivan and Gregor. The brothers now
flanked Kuschka, looking impatient to get on with business. Donning black leather jackets, the big, broad-
shouldered brothers stood like granite slabs, towering
over the seated Germans, their lean faces tight with intense anger.

"Is all this necessary, Herr Kuschka?" Furst
growled, gesturing at the Kalashnikovs.

"I believe it is. I have had some problems, and one
can never be too careful. I have seen your own security
detail around the chalet. They are heavily armed."

"So it would seem you have had problems," bank
vice president Peter Bauer said.

"I do not take being threatened by you lightly,"
Furst rasped.

Kuschka glanced at the skinny, balding man. "I trust
you have our money?"

"Your accounts have been closed as you wanted,"
Furst said. "One hundred million was wired to an account in the Philippines as you directed us to do."

There were pitchers of water on the table beside a
telephone and intercom. Kuschka noticed many of the
Germans were drinking water frequently, refilling their
glasses from the pitchers, straining, it seemed, to hide
their frayed nerves. Kuschka smelled the fear in the air.
He knew them by name, had done business with them
personally. Their reputations were something else entirely. They loved money and the good life, and they
didn't care how they had come by it or held on to it. If

they didn't do as he wished, they would lose everything, including their lives.

"It was not easy," Furst said, filling his water glass, drinking. "Funds had to be diverted—"

"I do not care how it was done! I do not want to hear about bearer bonds, stock investments and liquidation."

Furst grunted. "But, of course, as long as you have eighty million in American cash."

Kuschka's gaze narrowed. "You see me as a criminal, I understand. But, Comrades, it was you who took our money. My money helped build this chalet for you." A few of them grimaced. "I understand you have much to lose if my troubles become yours, which is why I insisted on this emergency meeting."

"We are men of money not men of a vision for a future of some new Russia," said Harvey Romerhof, Furst's lawyer.

"The future is one of unlimited wealth, but not in the manner in which the West was helping Russia. The supposed aid and investment, my German friends," Kuschka said, clasping his hands behind his back, "your bank was sending to Moscow was merely destined to fall into the hands of corrupt politicians. We made a deal from the very beginning. I invested money in your fledgling bank and made you the power you are. You reinvested my money in other endeavors, and we watched it grow. I am only interested in results."

"Your business is narcotics and arms dealing," Bauer said. "Unless we free ourselves of your money, we are sure to come under close scrutiny by Interpol."

Kuschka listened as Ivan Dmitrov growled in Russian, "Let's get our money from them. I cannot stand to look at this swine much longer."

Kuschka nodded; he couldn't agree more. "The money, gentlemen. From here on, once we leave your country, I assure you you need not worry about your futures."

Furst hit a button on the intercom. "Bring it in."

Kuschka waited. The giant oak doors opened. The entire security detail for the Germans was holding the money bags. Six large men in windbreakers, with Austrian AUG assault rifles slung across their shoulders, filed into the conference room. Twelve bulging duffel bags were dumped around Kuschka. The Russian pointed at four commandos, who moved from the wall. They zipped open each bag, displaying the rubber-banded stacks of U.S. hundred-dollar bills.

"This is unnecessary. It is all there!" Furst rasped.

"Take two of the bags. We can count it all later," Kuschka told Ivan Dmitrov, who then ordered one of his men to secure two bags.

"By the way, you had a phone call before you arrived. It was a man. He refused to identify himself or leave a message."

Kuschka peered at Furst, his heart skipping a beat. Only Svetlana or Tielig had the number for the chalet. Was it possible, he wondered, that the two Americans had tracked them to the chalet, were right then moving in, with subguns and rocket launchers?

"'By the way'? Why did you not tell me this sooner?" Kuschka snarled.

"It appeared you wished to get right to business. I assumed," Furst said, "it was one of your associates."

"You assumed wrong."

The phone rang suddenly. "I'll take that," Kuschka said, grabbing up the receiver. Instinct warned him it was his American nemesis who was on the other end. "Yes."

"The woman's dead," his nameless adversary told him, his voice as cold as ice, sounding as if it came from the bottom of a tomb. "You're next."

The American hung up. The dial tone buzzed like a hungry insect in Kuschka's ear. Svetlana had failed, he thought, but she had known the risks. Still he wondered what went wrong. Silently he cursed. He would miss her talent, both as an assassin and a woman, but he was forced to put her out of his mind. A plan of action taking shape in his mind, Kuschka told the Dmitrov brothers in Russian, "Someone is coming here who has caused me great trouble. Two men. They will be armed, and they will come in shooting."

"What?" Ivan Dmitrov said. "What are you saying? We've been followed by the law?"

"No, they are not acting in any official capacity. You have been paid back for the loss of your share of the merchandise. What I propose is that I give you another duffel bag full of money to stay behind and eliminate these men." They hesitated, but Kuschka knew their greed would cloud their judgment.

"Two men, you say?" Gregor Dmitrov said.

"Yes." Kuschka had seen the three executive choppers on the helipad on the north edge of the compound. He was torn between staying, avenging his lover's death, seeing to it personally that the Americans were eliminated. But he needed to be out of Germany, swiftly and safely. The Lebanon business with the Shiite terrorists was urgent, would turn the corner in his deal with the Pakistanis for the enriched plutonium and uranium.

"Another ten million waiting for you in Moscow upon the killing of these two men."

"Very well," Ivan Dmitrov said. "Consider it done."

Kuschka nodded. The chalet was moments from becoming an abattoir. The Russian needed those choppers. He had already contacted his crew who had transported the deadly nerve gas from the safehouse north of Munich. It was already loaded on the cargo plane. The money was now secured, but he needed the remaining balance of cash to complete his deal with the Pakistani colonel. It looked as if the agenda was falling securely in place.

He stepped back from the security detail, told the Dmitrov brothers to likewise stand back. When they were clear of the line of fire, Kuschka looked at his commandos and gave the order in Russian to kill the security force.

THROUGH HIS field glasses, Bolan surveyed the chalet. The gabled, large wooden structure sat high up on a ledge, basking beneath the sun. The snowcapped peaks of the Bavarian Alps loomed above the chalet. Bolan counted eight vehicles parked in the long front driveway. Strange, he thought, all those vehicles but no movement around the compound.

Bolan turned to Tielig, who was standing next to Grimaldi by the German's Lincoln.

"You say Furst has a security detail?"

Tielig nodded. "I already told you that. He always keeps six armed men on hand."

"What's wrong, Striker?"

Bolan looked at Grimaldi. They were grouped in a small clearing. Thick woods flanked the narrow dirt road that led up to the chalet. It had been an anxious run down the Autobahn from Munich, Bolan expecting to see flashing lights or a roadblock anytime. But they had cleared the garage of the killzone without being seen. The parking attendant, locked in his booth of thick glass reading a men's magazine, had given the three of them no more than a casual glance as he'd opened the gate. Jackley's body was left in the van, and Bolan had seen the blood and damage to the vehicle. Grimaldi had barely escaped with his life. In time someone would discover the bodies in Tielig's office suite, and the van. Before the authorities could begin an all-out manhunt for suspects in the killings, Bolan intended to be long gone from Germany. Even still he felt a sense of urgency, hoping their luck held.

"It's too quiet up there," Bolan told his friend.

"How do you want to approach the chalet?" Grimaldi asked.

"You say Furst usually flies here in a chopper?" Bolan asked Tielig.

"Yes."

"Well, I saw an area large enough to be a helipad. If he flew here, he's gone now."

Mentally Bolan ran back his cryptic phone call to Kuschka. Before that, Tielig had reached Furst's secretary at the World Bank Center. An important client, Tielig was then directed to call the chalet. It seemed Furst was in an important conference. Suspecting Kuschka was en route to gather his illicit funds, Bolan called back, reached out and touched a nerve in his Russian adversary.

Again surveying the chalet, Bolan suspected Kuschka had flown off in a chopper. Perhaps a trap was waiting for Bolan up there. All along the numbers had been falling into one cat-and-mouse engagement after another. Set up an ambush on the enemy, or be used as bait to flush them out. If nothing else, the two Stony Man warriors were shaving the odds with each enemy gun they silenced.

"I'm going up on foot," Bolan told Grimaldi. "You drive up as close as you can. Put Tielig in the trunk first."

"What? This is an outrage!"

"You brought this down on your own head, Tielig," Bolan told the German. "You've been helping to ship weapons of possible mass destruction and shipments of cash. You invested in a major narcotics deal and lost. It's time you took some accountability for your actions."

"I told you, I did not handle my business personally. It came to my attention only days ago that my planes have been used without my knowledge. It would appear Kuschka, Calhoun and the others were working with my employees behind my back."

"You're hardly innocent," Grimaldi said. "I'm sure you fattened your own bank account plenty—even with your hands-off style."

Tielig scowled. "Who are you men? You come into my country, bulldozing your way into my office, killing people, kidnap me, now you intend to kill even more people."

Bolan ignored the man. Depending on how the numbers fell, Tielig was leaving Germany with them. He would be handed over to blacksuits from the Farm once they were clear of Germany, taken back to Brognola to be thoroughly grilled for any information he could provide on his dealings with the enemy.

That was the game plan for the following day. Right then, Bolan needed to put full, grim focus on the chalet and whatever was up there waiting for him.

Removing his coat and opening the trunk, the Executioner reached for his combat webbing and harness.

IT WAS a grueling thirty-minute hike uphill, through thick woods, searching for a path that would allow him to silently approach the chalet without being seen.

Finally Bolan reached a rocky embankment and settled into a gully. He looked up at the large open porch on the back west end of the chalet, about thirty yards directly above. There was still no sign that anyone was inside the chalet. Bolan didn't like it. Over the countless years of probes, soft and hard recons of enemy compounds, he'd developed a sixth sense for unseen danger.

Someone, possibly a small army, was ready and waiting inside the chalet.

He snugged the Uzi submachine a little higher up on his shoulder. He contacted Grimaldi via his throat mike, quietly said, "I'm at the west end. It still looks deserted."

"I'm fifty yards down the driveway, parked in a thicket. Same thing from the east."

"Proceed with caution. Use the frag grenades to get inside if you have to. The closest village is six miles east. According to our intel, the chalet is just about as remote as that château in the Pyrenees."

"Making noise is the last thing I'm worried about."

"Good to hear. Watch yourself."

"Likewise."

Bolan disengaged communication. He was moving up the gully, his eyes on the railing, when three large figures moved out onto the patio. They toted AK-47s, wore black leather coats and they began to speak in Russian. They were looking around at the woods, two of the bigger Russians looking like twin mountains carved from granite. The twins moved back inside the chalet.

Bolan made his move on the lone sentry. He reached the top of the gully as the guard peered at the woods. The man's intense gaze was roving the Executioner's way, his eyes widening at the last possible second as he spotted the intruder below. Bolan squeezed the Beretta's trigger, and a whispering message of 9 mm death cored the sentry between the eyes. His head snapped back, a finger of blood jetting from the back of his skull on a burst of bone and brain matter, as Bolan made the steps.

The Executioner opted for his Uzi and cocked the bolt, chambering a round. The dead man hammered to the patio, the force and noise of his hard drop certain to alert any nearby enemies.

Bolan had sounded the alarm, and he wanted his enemies running out onto the patio to check the disturbance.

Seconds later two figures barreled onto the patio. The first goon spotted Bolan and swung his AK-47 toward the invader in black. The Executioner held back on the trigger of his Uzi, stitching the first gunman across the chest, left to right, a hammering burst that kicked the target backward. The other hardman jumped back for cover inside the doorway. Bolan's second target kept backing up, snarling something in Russian, his AK-47 rattling off rounds toward the sky. Finally the hardman pitched over the railing.

Bolan wheeled, watching two figures scurry into what looked like a kitchen beyond a giant stained-glass window. He ducked beneath the window as the two hardmen blasted out the glass with an extended barrage of AK-47 autofire.

The soldier armed a frag grenade as jagged sheets of glass blew over his outstretched form. He tossed the grenade through the teeth of the devastated window, and was up and running for the back doorway when the frag bomb detonated. The patio shook beneath the Executioner's feet as the blast blew out what remained of the stained-glass window. Uzi poised, he went in, hard and low.

He searched the twisted, smoking ruins of the large kitchen. One mangled figure looked pinned, facefirst, into the shattered ruins of a pantry. It was one of the twins.

Where was the other gunman?

An explosion sounded from the east end. Grimaldi was making his presence known with a fragmentation entrance. No sounds of gunfire, though. His friend, he hoped, was inside and clear.

Cautious, Bolan stepped into a narrow, winding hall, his Uzi fanning the gloom. He kicked open a door to his side, bursting into what looked to be a guest room, with a large bed and a dresser. He listened to the silence in the room, then heard a man shouting from somewhere to the west end in heavily accented English.

Moving out of the room, checking the rear, Bolan made his way to the sprawling living room, which was empty. As the soldier proceeded across the room, Grimaldi joined him.

"Shut up, or I'll kill all of you!"

Several people were shouting. The angry, frightened exchange came from beyond the open doorways off to one side of the living room.

On the fly, Bolan gave the living room and the wooden stairs leading to the second story a hard search. On the surface it appeared Kuschka had left behind a token force. But why? Why not throw everything he had at the two men who were hell-bent on hounding him to the ends of the earth to kill him and crush his insidious agenda?

Higher stakes in Lebanon, no doubt. It was the only thing that made sense to Bolan. Germany was a wash for Bolan, and merely a stepping-stone for Kuschka. Apparently the Russian had gotten the necessary funds from his moneymen. A terrorist army was waiting in Lebanon for the shipment of weapons of mass destruction.

Lebanon had to wait. The present demanded the full lethal concentration from both warriors.

As they closed on the doorway, then crouched on opposite sides, Bolan pointed at his eyes, indicating Grimaldi watch their rear while he dealt with whatever was beyond the doors. Looking just inside the doorway, Bolan found six bodies, riddled with bullet holes. He put the dead out of mind, then heard a voice shout from inside, "You, whoever you are! I have three very important and respected German businessmen, bound up like pigs for the slaughter! They are my hostages! We are all walking out of here!"

The voice came from deep inside the room. Peering low around the corner, Bolan spotted the second twin at the far end of a massive conference table. The enemy had a forearm locked around the throat of a stocky German. The other two hostages sat in swivel chairs beside the hardman and hostage, their eyes wide with terror. Bolan didn't see anyone else in the room, but that didn't mean gunmen weren't hugging the wall on either side. The big Russian held an AK-47 in a one-handed grip, the barrel aimed at the doorway.

"Sounds like you got your money and don't care if they live or die," Bolan said.

"You're right, I don't care. I have my money and I am leaving."

"What makes you think I care about them, either? They're as dirty as you are."

The enemy cursed in Russian. "Throw down your weapons now!"

Bolan pushed it. "No chance. You're not walking out of here."

Whether he was insane with fear or blood lust, Bolan didn't know. But the gunman gave the Executioner all the opening he needed in the next moment.

"I will show you how serious I am!" the big Russian shouted.

Suddenly the AK-47 blazed. The seated Germans took the barrage of 7.62 mm lead full in their faces. Bolan surged into the room. The surviving hostage broke free. Possibly enraged he had lost his edge, the Russian drilled a burst of lead into the German's back. As the businessman sailed in a nosedive for the floor, Bolan cut loose with his Uzi. Sliding off to one side as the big Russian tried in vain to track Bolan with AK autofire, the soldier poured it on with his Uzi. The wave of 9 mm slugs chewed the Russian's torso to crimson shreds. The Russian screamed, cursed in his native tongue, then plunged from Bolan's view.

Bolan reached the fallen German and recognized Hermann Furst, president of the bank that, according to Stony Man Farm intel, had laundered or channeled billions of illicit dollars for the drug-and-arms-dealing mercenary army of Hydra.

Bolan knelt, looked back and found Grimaldi standing guard in the doorway. He gave the German enough of a slap on the face to bring him back from the edge of death for the moment.

"Furst?"

The German grunted, trying to focus on Bolan.

"Where's Kuschka?"

"Bastard Russians...betrayed us...killed my people...."

Bolan repeated the question.

"Took our choppers...Tielig...I imagine..."

The German died with anger in his eyes.

The soldier rose and said, "Let's roll, Jack."

GOING BACK TO MUNICH, then making a run for the airport was one of the biggest gambles Bolan had taken in some time.

The midafternoon sun hung over the distant Munich skyline when Grimaldi drove the Lincoln Towncar up to the airfield's main office. There was no air traffic, landing or going. The airport appeared deserted, other than two men in white coveralls appearing to do some maintenance on a twin-engine plane on a grassy clearing near the office. The two men glanced at the Towncar, keeping their backs turned as they fiddled in toolboxes. The same suspicious feeling the soldier had experienced at the chalet was causing his combat instincts to flare. He believed Kuschka had flown off already, but suspected the Russian might have left behind another skeleton killing crew at Tielig's airfield.

The two warriors would find out if the enemy was lying in wait soon enough. Either way, they had made the home stretch in Germany. There were no official police vehicles waiting for them. Luck was holding.

Grimaldi braked the vehicle in front of the office building. Bolan opened his door and exited the back seat, hauling Tielig out of the car with him. "Stay calm. You're just taking a little ride with some business associates."

Instinct warned Bolan he wouldn't be able to bluster his way past Gortslip again. Tielig looked too frightened for the soldier to pull off another ruse.

The office door opened, and Gortslip ventured outside. Right away Bolan noted the change in the man's eyes, something hard, shadowy behind the German's stare.

"Herr Tielig? How are you today, sir?"

"Just fine, Herr Gortslip. My friend and I are going to take a little plane ride while we discuss business."

Gortslip hesitated, then told Bolan, "Your jet is fueled and ready to fly as you wished."

"Where is it?"

The man pointed at a lone hangar at the far north end of the airfield.

Bolan grew more suspicious. He shoved Tielig at Grimaldi, said, "Hold him tight."

As Grimaldi hauled in Tielig, Bolan drew his Beretta and aimed it at Gortslip, who sputtered, "What is the meaning of this?"

"Get over here now."

The German hesitated in the doorway.

"You can walk, or you can crawl if I shoot you in the knee."

Gortslip was moving toward Bolan when the soldier looked over his shoulder and saw the two maintenance men striding across the grassy clearing. Without a word they raised their submachine guns and began to fire. The attack happened so suddenly that neither Grimaldi nor Bolan could do much other than dive for cover. The ace pilot hit the ground while Bolan flung himself backward behind the front end of the Lincoln.

Unfortunately for Tielig, he was left fully exposed to the lightning sweep of subgun fire. Bolan saw the man take the full barrage of lead in the chest. As the German screamed in pain, spun and dropped on his back, Grimaldi came out of his roll, his Uzi up and firing at the two gunmen.

The Executioner flicked the selector switch on the Beretta 93-R to 3-round bursts, and the two warriors nailed the gunmen who had lost their advantage. The two would-be assassins became clear and close targets for the double punch of 9 mm lead that knocked them off their feet.

No sooner were they sprawled on the grass than Bolan was up and running for Gortslip. The German stumbled and pitched to the ground. Jacking Gortslip to his feet, Bolan thrust the silenced Beretta under his chin.

"How many in the hangar waiting for us?"

"T-two."

"Your life is depending on your answers. Has our jet been tampered with?"

"No. I swear."

"Where's Kuschka?"

"Flew off, maybe an hour ago in a cargo plane."

Bolan was fighting time. If Kuschka beat the Stony Man team to Lebanon, sealed their deal with terrorists on the other end, he might lose the enemy. He didn't think so, however. Bolan knew Brognola was hard at work, paving the way to get them into Lebanon to pick up the hunt.

First they needed to get to their jet, take care of the enemy in the hangar.

The distance to the hangar was roughly one hundred

yards. Most likely the enemy was watching, Bolan knew, since the sound of gunfire and the sight of the first hit team going down would have put them on full alert.

"They'll cut us down if we approach on foot," Grimaldi stated.

"We drive," Bolan said, forming a plan of attack. "Where exactly is the jet in the hangar?" he asked Gortslip.

"Directly behind the doors. It's the only aircraft inside."

"Side or back doors?"

"One in the back, one on each side."

"If we make the jet, you're flying with us, Gortslip. If there's a bomb on board, you go with us."

Bolan watched the man's expression harden with righteous indignation. "I told you, that jet has not been tampered with in any way."

Bolan believed him. Gortslip was too scared to not tell the truth.

The soldier took the keys, then hauled Gortslip to the back of the Towncar. Before the man could protest, Bolan opened the trunk and shoved him inside.

The soldier tossed the keys to Grimaldi. "You drive. This is how we'll handle it."

HE WANTED IT wrapped up, quick and clean, but Bolan knew that was far easier wished for than done.

Even still the soldier knew there was no other way than to go into the hangar, low and hard, take them as they showed. If necessary, he would frag them. If the jet suffered any damage during the engagement, Grimaldi would find some aircraft that would get them to their next destination, something, anything to fly them out of Germany.

As planned, Bolan hopped out of the Towncar and made the side door. Then Grimaldi raced the vehicle down the side of the hangar, wheeled hard and disappeared around the corner. Checking his watch, Bolan counted down the doomsday numbers. Thirty seconds and ticking off until he was in sync with Grimaldi.

Crouched by the side of the door, Uzi cocked and locked, Bolan listened but heard no sounds beyond his position.

When the numbers counted off, Bolan grabbed the door handle, turned it and opened the door. He peered around the corner and caught sight of a gunman with an AK-47 hunched beside a crate, dead ahead. Another voice shouted something indistinct in Russian from some point deeper in the hangar. Gunfire erupted from where that voice shouted in anger and alarm.

Bolan cut loose with his Uzi at the same instant his target opened up with his AK-47. The soldier dodged the tracking line of autofire, his own blaze of 9 mm lead stitching the crate, throwing wood splinters into the enemy's face. Taking cover behind a crate, Bolan spotted Grimaldi inside, the ace pilot darting behind a large bench with tools spread on its top.

The Executioner traded fire with his own target, then grabbed a frag grenade and armed it. The Learjet was parked, he discovered, roughly twenty yards from where Bolan's intended victim was concealed. It would be tricky, keeping the blast from reaching the jet, but the soldier aimed his throw for the far side of the crate, away from the jet. As the gunman wheeled around the crate, Bolan dropped the steel egg to his enemy's far left flank. The ensuing blast pulped the crate, sent the hardman sailing for the jet on a crunching fireball. His shredded body bounced off the sleek fuselage of the jet, then dropped to the floor.

Moving out, Bolan scanned the large hangar. So far there appeared no other gunman than the one trading autofire with Grimaldi. It looked as if Gortslip had told the truth, and Bolan felt reassurance that their jet was fueled and untouched by any form of sabotage.

The enemy saw Bolan racing across the hangar toward him. He shouted in Russian, his eyes wild with fear and rage as he realized he was caught in a cross fire. He started to swing his chattering AK-47 toward Bolan when both warriors mowed him down with a short scissoring burst of autofire.

"Get Gortslip," Bolan told Grimaldi. "I'll open the doors, and you check our jet."

Nodding, Grimaldi disappeared through the doorway. Bolan heard a groan of pain. He looked at the gunman they had just cut down. The man's chest was soaked with blood.

The Executioner loomed over the dying enemy. "Kuschka's flown on to Lebanon, hasn't he?"

"American, you will never catch him or defeat all of us...."

"So far that wouldn't seem entirely accurate."

Defiance hardened the Russian's eyes. "An entire army is in the Bekaa Valley. Another army is waiting...in Karachi...."

Bolan stared into the strange laughing look in the Russian's eyes.

"Go get yourselves killed. I just told you where to find them... I can rest in peace knowing I sent you to die by Kuschka's hand...."

The Russian sighed, then his head lolled to the side.

Lebanon. Pakistan. Kuschka had a full plate of pick-ups and deliveries. Well, Bolan intended to be on hand to make certain the surviving enemy hordes choked on their own blood.

15

Lebanon

Since the stinging backlash of humiliation and failure that had dogged them since Manhattan, Ben Calhoun felt is if everyone were giving him the evil eye these days. Failure. Defeat.

Huge sums of money were being wired all over the world, from Paris, Germany, the Bahamas to the East. His ex-KGB counterpart was scrambling to shore up the details for cash transactions and weapons shipments while they sat on their hands, wondering and worrying about their futures, even their lives. Now they were being treated to scowls and glares from Islamic terrorist scum. Calhoun was just about to snap, start kicking the closest ass any second.

Right then he had a full house of targets.

Sitting in the stone hut with his men, Calhoun had nothing but time to reflect on the mishaps and fiascos, brood about and size up the present, weigh the future.

There wasn't much promise that things would swing back their way. Unless, of course, they used deadly force. But against whom? The terrorists? Was Kuschka seeing his American comrades as expendable? When would the mystery enemy show again? Was Kuschka even alive?

Calhoun was down to ten men—literally, he thought, the last of a dying breed. Earlier they had landed at a remote makeshift airfield in the fertile, green Bekaa Valley. Then they had been moved by transport truck to an isolated village near the foothills of the Anti-Lebanon Mountains by a terrorist group that was protected by a unit of the Lebanese army, obviously paid off by either the terrorists or Kuschka or both to secure their haven. He recognized the blue uniforms and red berets of the Lebanese army, had seen the Russian T-54 tanks, four in all, and figured the paid-off Lebanese soldiers numbered roughly forty. Long odds, if it came to a firefight. Calhoun hoped Kuschka showed soon, hoped the deal went down without a hitch, hoped they flew on, safe and secure, to Karachi. A lot of hoping, he decided. Too much. A show of force was in the cards; he was sure of it. Suddenly there were too many players in the game, everyone with his own agenda.

Despite all the setbacks, the havoc wreaked on them by the enemy, Kuschka never failed to amaze Calhoun. The Russian appeared connected wherever they went, but he knew Kuschka had successfully transacted major arms deals with various terrorist groups in Lebanon before.

At the moment Calhoun and his surviving force were watched by a small army of Shiite Muslims. The terrorists were armed with AK-47s and RPG rocket launchers. Calhoun and his men, however, had been left with their Ingrams, Uzis, Berettas or Colt .45s, and their fighting knives. If it was some show of good faith on the part of the terrorist leader, Mohammed Huzbah, well, Calhoun wasn't believing in much these days other than his raging need to kill the first bastard who twitched a weapon his way.

How long had they been there, since flying from Germany in the Russian's private jet? A harrowing flight, refueling at a remote airfield in Turkey where grim-faced men with AK-47s had said nothing to the Russian pilots. From his window he had seen the duffel bag change hands. More payoffs. But that's the way it had been falling since he'd first met Kuschka in Vietnam. Money to buy silence, cooperation, to ship drugs and weapons, buy secrets from the CIA—or McBain.

Years of countless illicit deals became a jumbled maze of treachery and countertreachery in Calhoun's mind.

Running guns and drugs had made both of them fortunes, indeed, but all along he now saw it was merely a means to an end. More recently there had been the short stint where Calhoun and his ex–Special Forces soldiers had hired themselves to act as assassins for a renegade CIA paramilitary operation meant to wipe out terrorists in the Middle East. That was the problem. Beirut, where they had recently assassinated a rival splinter faction of the PLO, had been a fiasco. Getting into the terrorist safehouse, they had executed the targets, but out in the street all hell had broken loose. To secure their escape, Calhoun and his men had killed countless innocent Lebanese men, women and children while battling a backup force of terrorists from what turned out to be a rival PLO group who had been lying in ambush.

The tall, wiry, bearded Huzbah would frequently treat Calhoun to a piercing stare, as if racking his memory, wondering where he'd seen the Americans before.

Six Shiite terrorists were in the large, Spartanly furnished room. Elsewhere in the stone hovel and around the perimeter Calhoun figured there were close to forty more armed fanatics. Huzbah, Calhoun saw, was again giving him a scathing look, then moved off into another room where Calhoun had seen a large radio console.

It was dark outside, and according to Calhoun's watch, adjusted during the flight to Lebanese time, it was almost midnight. It could be hours before Kuschka landed with the new, deadly nerve agent. *If* Kuschka had even made it out of Germany. No news, he figured, was good news.

Although everywhere they went it seemed as if there was nothing but bad news and very bad news.

He was beginning to think of their enemy as very bad news.

Calhoun found the bulk of his force, sitting on chairs or the couches, smoking, cleaning their weapons. Only Augustly and Bittertown sat with Calhoun at the wooden table.

"How come I get the feeling we're on our own?" Augustly asked quietly.

"Kuschka will be here," Calhoun answered. "He has no choice but to seal this deal. These dung-eaters need that shipment so they can 'bring Israel to its knees.' We've got fifteen million in cash waiting to be picked up from them. That money will go, of course, to our Pakistani colonel. Too much is at stake for Kuschka to drop this deal."

"The only thing that's certain is more uncertainty," the squat, muscular Bittertown said. "I've seen the way Kuschka looked at us. As if we're the ones who are dangerous."

"I'm beginning to think we were better off on our own," Augustly said. "I don't trust our Russian comrades."

"No way. We need to stick with them. We've made too many enemies here, in the States, hell, everywhere except Russia. Don't forget we took money and assignments from guys in the CIA who worked with counterterrorism intelligence officers inside the Pentagon who fell during the late senator's grandstand on the Hill. There's no turning back.''

Bittertown scoffed. ''Makes me wonder how we've been found and tracked after years of staying invisible.''

''Someone behind bars squawked, that's for damn sure. How else could we have been picked and damn near annihilated in New York?'' Augustly growled.

''The CIA's known about us for several years. Anybody could have pointed the finger our way,'' Calhoun said, looking to calm their nerves.

They fell silent. Calhoun silently urged Kuschka to show so they could get on with business and be gone from Lebanon.

He couldn't help but wonder what the future held, if they were all doomed for defeat and death. In the beginning they had gone for the cash, and in a large way it was cleaner where only money was involved. Now it was about glory, a vision of a new world. They would commit mass genocide on selected weaker nations. Deposed dictators, he knew, from several African nations were now in exile, guarded by guns sent from Kuschka's superiors in the Coalition.

The near future would see mercenary armies storm the Kremlin, palaces in African nations, which would come under chemical, biological and nuclear blackmail. There was even a plan to nuke selected oil fields in the Middle East. Of course, Calhoun knew the logistics were still being ironed out, but it was going to happen. Meanwhile their global sweep would carry on, with Calhoun and Kuschka picking up mercenary armies to be used as the frontline soldiers in the coming world revolution.

For a long moment, Calhoun stared at the wooden shutters that had been closed over the window. Outside the green expanse of the Bekaa Valley held the site for what he hoped was the key turning point in their operation. What was it about the Bekaa, though, that was of special historic interest? Then it hit him. The Bekaa, according to biblical scholars, was supposed to be the stage for Armageddon where the forces of good and evil met to determine the fate of humankind. How and when it would happen was a mystery. He briefly recalled his years in a Catholic school, before he had become a "reformed" Catholic, disposing of the notion of a God, choosing not to believe in anything other than power of his own will. Money equalled ultimate power, he had seen, and those who controlled the wealth made the world go around. Money was god.

He had the money, but now they needed the power to control the destiny of humankind. Would their combined American-Russian force, along with the mercenary armies they had yet to round up, eventually be the catalysts for the ultimate battle to reshape the world in the image they wanted? If there was such a thing as the Four Horsemen of the Apocalypse, then perhaps they were it. Death. War. Famine. Plague. Gathering revolutionary armies, while the best minds in medicine, nuclear physics, bioengineering were working around the clock in a remote compound in the Russian Far East to create agents of mass destruction in every form conceivable: viruses that would wipe out both humans and food supplies; nuclear warheads, and nuclear backpacks to be launched or carried into targeted cities; aerosol with biological or chemical agents to hit Third World countries or any of these new republics in Russia. Anarchy, revolution, chaos and wholesale genocide were on the horizon.

It was time for a new world. Right then, knowing it had all reached critical mass, Calhoun wanted to believe, more than ever, in his destiny as a man who would rule his own country. Promises had been made by Kuschka, after all. McBain would also have his own country. Yes, unlimited power, glory and pleasure, he thought. Someday soon they would be gods among mere mortals.

"What happened to Abu?"

Calhoun was jolted back to the present. He found Huzbah standing in the doorway, a menacing look in his eyes.

"How do you know about Abu?"

"A brother in the jihad had seen you in Beirut, perhaps a year ago. You were recruiting for some attack on the infidels. What and how I know is not important. I know that Abu and the others didn't return from the land of the Great Satan."

With all the informants, intelligence agents from the CIA and Mossad, with all the different terrorist groups operating in and around Lebanon, it didn't surprise, nor did it matter that he was known to have recruited his terrorist army here.

"Abu and the others were paid well by me to attack New York," Calhoun answered.

"They are all dead?" Huzbah asked.

Was the terrorist tightening his grip on his assault rifle? Calhoun wondered.

"Yes. They knew the risks. They died, killing many infidels. I'm sure they went to Paradise."

Huzbah bared his crooked teeth. "You sound as if you mock us."

"I'm hardly in a position to do that," Calhoun said, tensing to sweep up his Ingram on the table in front of him.

"You made it back here alive."

"Barely."

Huzbah nodded. "I have many brothers in Beirut. I will check into this personally. Should I find there was some treachery or deceit on your part, then I will avenge their deaths."

Calhoun felt his heart race, watched as Huzbah left the room and gave the order for his brothers to join him. When they were alone, Calhoun ran a hard look over the faces of his men and said, "Be ready. If it looks like we're on our own, or about to go down, I suggest we make the most ferocious fighting withdrawal we're capable of."

To a man, they nodded. If they were destined to make one last stand, then Calhoun believed they could create a hell on earth that would rival anything the mythic Four Horsemen could unleash. After all, he thought, they were gods of war.

THE TWENTY BLACKSUITED commandos filed out of the tent. Bolan and Grimaldi sat at the large wooden table in the temporary command post on the Israeli-Lebanon border. Both men were dressed in combat blacksuits, complete with webbing and harness, with side arms and frag grenades. M-16s with M-203 grenade launchers were canted against their legs. Intent, both Stony Man warriors watched the special operative from the CIA. The big, broad-shouldered, crew-cut man, who had just given the final briefing, was Major Bill Towers.

As the major ran a dark gaze over the two men, Bolan gave silent thanks to the speedy and well-organized path Brognola had laid out. From Germany a temporary refueling site had been hastily erected by Stony Man Farm in southern Italy. After they had landed on the makeshift airfield, Gortslip had been turned over to the blacksuits from the Farm. The German would be whisked back to the States for interrogation by Brognola. If the big Fed learned anything of value about the enemy's operations from Gortslip, he would inform Bolan ASAP. At the moment Brognola was laying the groundwork for the two warriors to get into Pakistan. More shadow enemies, involved in the Hydra conspiracy, were waiting there, Bolan knew, but first they needed to deal with the sale of chemical weapons to terrorists in the Bekaa Valley.

And during the flight to Israel, Bolan had received his orders from the big Fed. Brognola had used his contacts in the CIA to get Bolan and Grimaldi aboard a covert Company operation that had apparently known about and been tracking Calhoun for some time. Towers knew about the deal between Calhoun, Kuschka and the terrorists in the Bekaa Valley. Whether it was luck or fate, Bolan and Grimaldi had been attached to the commando operation to nail Calhoun and whatever other enemy numbers were holed up in the Bekaa. Bolan suspected Kuschka would also be on hand for the dawn strike.

Towers cleared his throat. ''I get the impression from my superiors that you two are a whole lot more than Special Agents Belasko and Griswald from the Justice Department. Be that as it may, from what you've told me about how you've been hunting Calhoun and this Russian KGB killer since that suicide terrorist attack on

Manhattan, I gather that this thing has turned personal for the both of you.''

Bolan looked the man square in the eye. ''This isn't about vengeance, Major. We keep personal feelings out of this. This is about a conspiracy, within and beyond our own government, that has been shaping up for years. It would certainly appear it has reached critical mass. I'll allow that to some degree it is about justice.''

Towers grunted. ''All I know is you two must be pretty damn important for me to give you carte blanche and act in joint command of this operation. Understand, it's been months of using informants, Mossad and CIA agents inside Beirut to get wind of this deal. The Israeli government, because of what happened on American soil, has granted us a window of time to deal with these bastards in the Bekaa. My informants and my sat recon have clearly determined the target site. You, Agent Griswald, can go ahead and command one of the Hueys.''

''He would be of better assistance for the ground-and-air strike if he could command an Apache,'' Bolan said.

''The Huey will have to do. I've got my own pilots for the two Apaches. Plus you wanted your own four-man team, Belasko. This is going to have to go down by the numbers. With Calhoun in this village, an army of thirty-plus Shiite fanatics, not to mention the backing of the Lebanese army, it's going to get damn ugly.''

''The CIA has known about Calhoun for some time, haven't they?'' Bolan asked.

''Yes. I hope you're not implying we've got a shit-load of conspirators walking among my ranks.''

''I was just wondering how Calhoun has been able to do what he's been doing all these years.''

''So have we. It isn't hard to understand, though.''

Towers squared his shoulders. "Money buys silence and strange bedfellows. Calhoun and McBain, the treasonous bastard, have somehow slipped through the cracks. As for the Manhattan suicide attack, unfortunately, it's sort of like a cop getting to the scene of the crime after the fact. We can't know everything. I don't want to rehash ancient history.

"It would certainly seem that after years of our targets moving at large and conducting their illicit business, they've compiled more money than most Third World countries. They covered their tracks, bribed, killed and generally just kicked ass around the world. Where a former KGB assassin fits in, well, the CIA knows there's an entire organization of former military, intelligence people, GRU, old hard-line political leaders, who have been conspiring for a long time to begin a new revolution in the motherland."

Bolan figured he had very little choice right then other than to ride with the major's program. Given the enemy numbers they were facing, Bolan knew it would take everything the major could throw at the enemy to finally bring them down.

"One other thing," Towers said. "We take no prisoners. If it's armed, I don't care if it's a twelve-year-old kid with a knife, it goes down and stays down."

"You said this stretch of the valley is entirely controlled by the terrorists who are being protected by the Lebanese army."

"The village belongs lock, stock and barrel to the terrorists. There won't be civilian casualties, if that's what you're worried about, Belasko."

"You've got what," Grimaldi said, "four Russian T-54 tanks, two Mi-24 Hind gunships at this compound ten klicks north of the village. Two Apaches and three

Hueys, and a little over twenty of us going after maybe sixty, seventy enemy numbers. Factor in Calhoun and Kuschka's people, we may be looking at another twenty to thirty guns. What about antiaircraft artillery?''

"You two don't strike me as ones who'd get cold feet."

"Merely assessing the situation, Major," Grimaldi said.

"We hit them hard, from the air and the ground. There's no indication the targets have antiaircraft capability. You've got your assignments. If they scatter, we track them. From what I've learned from my informant and sat recon, there's a gorge, almost right between the village and the Lebanese army compound, that's been secured, and it looks like they're setting up a runway. I suspect that's where the transaction will take place."

"What do you know about this nerve agent?" Bolan asked.

"It came from a compound in South Africa. The CIA worked hard with the South African authorities to raid this compound. A week ago we picked up and interrogated a team of bioengineers, chemists who turned out to be working for Kuschka. The agent had already been shipped out, but we got a sample. It's a botulinum toxin, but other agents we've yet to determine were added to it. It has a bonus factor, if you will, that creates an effect similar to the Ebola virus. Aside from muscular paralysis, then asphyxiation, the victim burns up from fever, the blood boils, flooding from every orifice of the body. It appears a combination chem-bio agent. Whether the agent is contagious, well, we don't know much more at this time."

"These are Shiite fanatics," Bolan said. "If their

back is to the wall and this nerve agent is on hand, they'll use it."

"You'll get protective masks to fix to your webbing once you're on board."

"What about a MOPP suit?" Grimaldi asked.

"I don't think you'll need a Mission Oriented Protective Posture suit."

"You don't think?" Grimaldi said.

"It's too cumbersome to be running around in a biohazard suit, Griswald. From what our own scientists have learned about the nerve agent, it has to be breathed, not absorbed by the skin to work."

"You hope," Grimaldi said. "You yourself said they don't know that much about it."

"I don't want to see this strike get to the point where we have to find out. I know you gentlemen are looking beyond to a certain Pakistani colonel, but I suggest you give full attention to what's going on here."

"We wouldn't have it any other way, Major," Bolan said.

"Good. Anything else you want to discuss, we do it on the way. The sun's just about to come up. Let's go, gentlemen."

Standing, Bolan and Grimaldi hauled up their assault rifles.

16

Three continents, three times as many disasters and
countless dead later, it looked as if a major deal would
finally get launched, cash in hand for the home team.

It was Kuschka's show. The Americans could do little but let the Russians, terrorists and Lebanese soldiers
take center stage, determine everyone's immediate
future.

If nothing else, Calhoun's confidence was bolstered
that the Russians had landed. Despite a nagging fear
that anything could go wrong at any time, Calhoun
knew his Russian counterparts, armed to the teeth,
would get them clear of Lebanon if it hit the fan. Even
still, given everything that had happened up to that
point, Calhoun trusted nothing at face value, was ready
to start shooting any second.

The unmarked Antonov transport had rolled to a stop
only minutes earlier, after touching down beyond the
mouth of the gorge in a makeshift airfield lined with
flares. Calhoun, his Ingram slung across his shoulder,
watched from just beyond the transport as Huzbah's fanatics hauled several crates from the Antonov.

Standing alone with his men, with nothing to do but
wait and worry, Calhoun sized the situation. Maybe
thirty Lebanese soldiers were grouped around transport
trucks, Land Rovers and Jeeps in the mouth of the

gorge. Shiite terrorists were spread up the sides of the gorge, armed shadows in gullies or perched behind trees. The barrels of assault rifles poked out from behind trunks on Calhoun's flanks. Sentries were positioned on the ridges of the gorge, north and south, with a radio team on either side.

The commanding officer of the Lebanese unit, Colonel Birakah, a lean, mustachioed man with an AK-47 slung across his shoulder, was inspecting the transaction as Shiite fanatics opened the crates.

Calhoun didn't like the whole setup. Factor in two monster T-54 tanks in the mouth of the gorge, figure they were outgunned, six, maybe seven or eight to one by the Lebanese soldiers and the Shiites...well, if Huzbah and the Lebanese colonel turned their guns on them, it would be all they could do to fight their way out of the gorge. Calhoun hoped that didn't happen. Pakistan waited.

This was only the first of the next two major deals.

A dozen or so flares sizzled around the Antonov. Dawn, he figured, was less than an hour away. A low wind howled through the gorge, the ghostly whisper fraying his nerves even more. No, Calhoun didn't trust the darkness, the fact that all had been so quiet up to that point. There was an itch between his shoulder blades, the kind of feeling he got when he knew an enemy was lurking. The specter of the mystery enemy kept fleeting through his mind.

It was different this time, though, and again Kuschka amazed him.

Apparently Kuschka was prepared in case they were hit from the air. In a pocket near the mouth of the gorge, a tracked vehicle had wheeled in a Russian ZSU-23-4. The antiaircraft artillery had four self-propelled, quad-barreled, 23 mm automatic cannons. Two of Kuschka's finest manned the cannon.

There were other surprises also. Either as a bonus prize or reassurance, Kuschka had passed out six SAM-7 antiaircraft missile launchers. Calhoun had seen the weapon at work in Vietnam, Afghanistan and the Middle East and had sold more than a few SAM-7s over the years to various terrorist groups himself. The SAM-7 could launch an HE heatseeker warhead, capable of locking on to aircraft exhaust and streaking for a target at Mach 1.5.

They were ready in case the sky dropped on them again.

Calhoun listened to the exchange between Kuschka and Huzbah.

"You have ten thousand warheads," the ex-KGB killer told the Shiite leader as Huzbah picked up and inspected a cone-shaped warhead from the crate. "As I promised, they are designed to fit to an RPG rocket launcher. You also have five thousand canisters. Simple enough to use. Pull the pin, and you have a one-minute time delay before the toxin is dispersed. My suggestion would be to secure positions with the wind to your backs."

"Very primitive devices," Huzbah said. "I am still hoping for missiles that can be launched from a tracked vehicle."

"It was the best I could do on short notice. What you see is perhaps primitive, but very effective. How you get them into Israel is your affair."

"They'll get into Israel, believe me."

"Somehow, I do," Kuschka said.

"Why do I get the feeling, Comrade Kuschka," the

Lebanese colonel said, gesturing at the SAM-7s, then nodding at the ZSU-23-4, "you fear an attack?"

The Russian's scarred face looked especially hideous to Calhoun right then, bathed in the glow of the flares. It didn't escape Calhoun's observation the blond woman hadn't landed with Kuschka. Something had gone wrong in Germany. The woman was dead, he suspected. The mystery enemy had struck again.

"I do not fear an attack," Kuschka stated. "I only wish to be prepared in the event of trouble. I will not lie to you. We have had trouble. We are being hunted, even as we speak, but I expect our transaction will go off smoothly and we will be gone in short order."

"You assured us we would have no fear of an attack!" Huzbah snarled.

"I assured you nothing. It was you who assured me we could land. It was you who assured me you had this area clear of both Israelis and any Syrian army patrols. For the Lebanese to operate in this part of the Bekaa tells me you control it without Syrian interference."

"I assure you we are in complete control," Birakah said. "You advanced us cash to pay off the necessary Syrian officers. They are soldiers whom I know personally, and they wish the same thing as the rest of us. The destruction of Israel."

"Speaking of cash, gentlemen," Kuschka said, "I believe it is time to pay up."

"I would prefer a demonstration of a warhead first."

Kuschka stiffened. "What would you suggest? We stay here until you find a Bedouin tribe to attack? Do you doubt these weapons are what I say they are?"

Huzbah balked. "No. Very well, we have done business before. You have always come through for us."

"Indeed. So what would be different now?"

Calhoun watched as Huzbah barked an order, and two armed shadows pulled large satchels from inside a Jeep. They were moving toward the transport plane when Calhoun found himself under the angry scrutiny of Huzbah.

"How well do you know your American comrade, the major?"

Kuschka seemed puzzled by the question. "What do you mean?"

"Some disturbing information has reached me by way of my own informants in Beirut. It would appear he recruited a Palestinian named Abu for a suicide mission that recently occurred in New York City. It would appear he used fellow brothers in our holy war as cannon fodder to achieve some aim of his. It would appear he also was part of a covert commando operation that wiped out many Iranians and other warriors in the jihad a little while back in Beirut. Many innocent women and children died during his escape. I have to believe he was perhaps paid very well for both of these operations. I would believe he is—how do you say?—playing both ends against the middle. I ask you now," Huzbah said to Kuschka, "would you leave the Americans behind until I can verify these facts or interrogate them myself?"

Calhoun believed he actually saw Kuschka thinking about doing just that. Calhoun waited for an answer that would determine if he and his men lived or died.

Finally Kuschka said, "I cannot do that. These men are part of my ongoing operation."

Huzbah injected ice into his voice. He barked an order, and the two Shiites with the money stopped beside him.

"What about for your money?"

Kuschka was baring his teeth, when a Lebanese soldier shouted from the mouth of the gorge, a radio mike in his hand, "Five attack helicopters just flew over the village. They are headed this way!"

IT WAS Towers's operation, for the most part, but Bolan knew how severely things changed in the heat of all-out combat. Something was warning the Executioner the surgical strike wasn't going down by the numbers.

Up to then, the two Stony Man warriors had inflicted heavy casualties on the enemy. Once, twice, even three times they had gotten away with lightning air and ground strikes. Sooner or later the enemy would prepare itself with something other than numbers and subguns or assault rifles.

Towers had sounded too confident during the briefing, Bolan recalled. A surprise, he suspected, was waiting for them. Factor in that the CIA hadn't gotten even an inkling about the Manhattan siege, and Bolan knew there could an oversight here.

The soldier stared over the shoulder of the door gunner, past the M-60 machine gun. Through his infrared binoculars, he saw the head-clothed figures with weapons, taking cover behind the stone wall ringing the village. Brief pencil-tip flames shot from those assault rifles, but the gunships were already well out of effective range.

The Huey that carried Bolan, Grimaldi and the five blacksuited commandos flew the outer left wing of the gunship formation. Ahead the Apaches flew point, and Bolan glimpsed them streaking on through the inky darkness. East, the first rays of dirty gray light were breaking over the horizon.

Bolan was moving for the cockpit when Towers patched through on his earpiece.

"Belasko, come in!"

Bolan spoke into his throat mike. "Belasko here. What have you got, Major?"

"The targets are in the gorge. I've got troop movement on the south ridge, sentries. Ground personnel are scrambling for positions. The T-54s are cranking up, gun barrels aimed our way, twelve o'clock."

Bolan stared past Grimaldi, through the cockpit Plexiglas. Less than one mile and closing hard, he saw the Apaches go to work. Hellfire missiles streaked away from the wings of the gunships.

"Break off for your assignment!" Towers told Bolan. "Let's nail these bastards! Copy that!"

"That's affirmative, Major."

"Get busy and don't let me down! Over and out!"

"The major says for us to go to work," Bolan told Grimaldi, who nodded.

As Grimaldi banked away from the formation, Bolan saw the mouth of the gorge light up with explosions. Vehicles were sent soaring on balls of fire.

Only the enemy proved Bolan's hunch right. Return fire was instant, heavy and accurate.

The monster Russian tanks boomed out their payloads, and Bolan spotted through his binoculars a multibarreled cannon pounding away at the gunships. Grimaldi was veering the Huey hard to the west when one Apache and a Huey blossomed into thundering fireballs.

The enemy was prepared this time.

THE EXECUTIONER disembarked from the Huey with his commando team, landing on the ridge with catlike grace, his M-16 poised to fire. Down in the gorge the soldier found all-out war had erupted. Dark shadows were blazing away at the gunships that swept over the gorge. They were firing with automatic weapons from both sides, along the ridge and from the mouth of the gorge. They were covered behind Jeeps and Land Rovers, or taking up positions near the transport plane.

Gunships kept unloading with 30 mm chain-gun fire and rocket fire. Blinding fireballs marched through the mouth of the gorge, shredding man and machine. But the gunships were forced to fly on, past the north ridgeline to evade the cannon fire and the T-54s.

As previously planned, Bolan knew their own assignment was to hit the target from behind while the other gunships formed a pincer assault on the enemy. Only the home team was down to three gunships. Grimaldi had flown in low, dropping the gunship below the south ridge while flying on to the west end of the gorge. Hugging the ridge was the only thing that might have saved them from the barrage of enemy cannon fire that kept hammering the sky.

In the distance, beyond the giant transport plane, Bolan recognized the cannon as a Russian ZSU-23-4.

The soldier was forced to concentrate on his own predicament.

Armed shadow figures charged up the hill toward him. The Executioner and his commandos spread out. In unison five M-16s cut loose. Autofire scythed through the enemy gunners below.

Grimaldi sent the gunship down the slope. The M-60 door gunner swept the hillside with long, raking bursts. Beyond the thunderclaps of explosions and the shriek of heavy lead off stone, the soldier heard the cries of pain as the ace pilot and the door gunner scored deadly hits.

Return fire forced Bolan to dart behind a tree halfway down the slope. Something streaked up from the gorge. In the grayish green tint of his NVD goggles, Bolan glimpsed the warhead a millisecond before it blew among their ranks. Two blacksuited figures to Bolan's flank were hurled back up the slope. The soldier's ears rang from the blast, as he hugged the ground, smoke and stone shrapnel blowing over his head.

Towers raised Bolan as the soldier saw one of the T-54s take a direct hit from a Hellfire missile.

"Belasko, come in! Are you in position from the west?"

"Belasko here, that's affirmative. I'm halfway down the slope."

"I need that antiaircraft battery taken out ASAP! I've spotted crates around that transport plane. If at all possible, I don't want that plane touched. An explosion could set off the nerve gas. You copy, Belasko?"

"That's affirmative."

"I can't risk losing another chopper, and we're under serious fire up here! Get Griswald on that cannon! We'll make strafing runs over the gorge, but I need that cannon taken out!"

"We're on it," Bolan said, forced to shout over the din of weapons fire and the distant crunch of explosions and thundering of cannons. "Over and out."

Bolan patched through to Grimaldi. "Can you get a shot at the ZSU?"

"I've got at least twenty Shiites hugging the foot of this gorge, some armed with RPGs."

"I'll cover you. Take out that cannon!"

"Roger."

As the Huey soared away, its rotor wash kicking up funnels of dust and grit, Bolan gave the order to his commandos to move out. Firing their M-16s at maybe ten targets directly below, Bolan leapfrogged ahead, using the cover of trees and boulders, enemy lead scorching the air around him.

Bolan armed a frag grenade and hurled it at a group of three fanatics in a gully below. Shouting and cursing reached his ears before the frag bomb blew, hurling shredded bodies in all directions.

The Executioner and his two commandos made their move to reach the gorge. Two shadows popped up on his flank as the ground leveled out. Wheeling, Bolan dropped them with an extended burst of 5.56 mm lead. An RPG flew away from a tumbling Shiite's hands. Above, Bolan glimpsed the Huey hugging the ridgeline. Minigun fire flamed from the chopper, stitching gunmen on the ridge, kicking them down the slope.

Bolan saw the other Huey touch down along the south ridge. Eight blacksuits were disembarking just as the ZSU-23-4 nailed the gunship. Blacksuits nose-dived to the ridge as yet another mushroom cloud of fire lit the gorge. The fireball swept up at least two of the commandos, hurtling them off the ridge on its screaming tongue of fire.

Bolan held back on the trigger of his M-16, heard the deafening chatter of his commandos unleashing autofire on shadows scrambling away from the transport. Downrange men screamed, whirled, died.

Ramming a fresh 30-round magazine into the M-16, Bolan lined up grim death sights on three Shiite fanatics. Dead ahead of him the trio was lifting RPG-7s to down the Huey.

Grimaldi was coming in on the blind side of the two-man crew manning the ZSU-23-4. The ace pilot loosed a barrage of rockets as Bolan dropped the RPG team with a sustained burst of M-16 autofire.

It wasn't a second too soon, Bolan saw, as he spotted two warheads flying past the rear of the Huey.

Moving into the gorge, the soldier searched for targets.

KUSCHKA KNEW there was still a window of opportunity to escape the conflagration all around him. The antiaircraft battery could cover their fighting withdrawal, but only for so long.

He was outraged once again that the enemy had swept over them, out of nowhere, threatening annihilation. Grim questions danced through his mind, questions that locked on his thoughts even as men died and explosions shook the gorge and launched wreckage around him. The enemy either had superior intelligence, was capable of tracking them wherever they went or there was an informant among the Coalition. Or maybe the enemy was snagging wounded prisoners along the way, forcing his people to talk and lay out their next move.

Whatever, the Russian had to force his undivided attention back to the raging battle at hand.

It was design, rather than luck, that had his ZSU-23-4 raking the sky and holding off the gunships as he led his Spetsnaz troops for a Land Rover and two Jeeps still intact. Reaching the Lebanese command post was critical. Then he saw Calhoun and his soldiers rolling up on his flank. The Americans were firing away with their subguns at the sky, but Kuschka knew they'd never pierce the armor plating of the lone Apache gunship as it soared over the mouth of the gorge.

Kuschka hauled in the discarded satchels from the dead Shiites who had just been cut down by cannon fire from the Huey unloading its troops on the south ridge. An eye blink later that Huey was history as his ZSU-23-4 crew raked the gunship with an extended barrage.

Misfortune struck yet again.

The other Huey, Kuschka saw, hugging the north ridge, vaporized his antiaircraft battery with rocket fire hitting them from the rear. With metal and body parts flying all over the gorge, Kuschka, crouched and running, turned and spotted the enraged face of Huzbah. The terrorist was racing up on his flank, his AK-47 swinging up.

"You bastard!" Huzbah raged. "You knew this was going to happen!"

Autofire rang out, a long barrage that clearly knifed through the distant chatter of weapons fire on Kuschka's rear.

As Huzbah's corpse dropped to the ground, Kuschka found Calhoun and his men, weapons smoking, and raced past the fallen man.

Calhoun wore a grim smile. "That was for going to bat for us, Comrade."

"We must reach the command post. I will radio ahead and get the Hinds airborne."

"Where's the jet?" Calhoun shouted.

All around him Lebanese soldiers and scattered bands of Shiites were holding the gorge. They would die, of course, but their fanaticism might get them clear of the gorge and to the jet. Or so Kuschka hoped.

"Get in the Jeep!" Kuschka ordered Calhoun.

Ahead, Kuschka found the lone T-54 swinging its cannon, attempting to line up target acquisition on the Apache as it swept over the mouth of the gorge.

Kuschka realized if they cleared the gorge it would be a miracle. Stranger things had happened, he thought, and reached the Land Rover that held his money.

17

Mop-up of the enemy wasn't guaranteed.

Flanked by his two-man commando team, Bolan reached the transport plane's tail. Crouching, the soldier took in the battle, assessing the situation, determining his next move. Everywhere, it seemed, Shiites were still holding their ground, AK-47s chattering in their hands as they fired at the shadows of the American commandos on the south ridge. Scattered pockets of the enemy had taken cover in gullies along the foothills to the south, or were firing away from near the mouth of the gorge. Apparently Bolan and his commandos, with a little help from his ace pilot, had secured the north side with total decimation of the enemy.

Ahead, Bolan saw armed shadows stretched out in prone positions near flaming wreckage. A quick burst from his M-16, and he took out two Shiites near the fiery hull of an overturned Jeep.

The problem of the nerve gas grabbed Bolan's concern. A hard, sweeping surveillance of the killzone revealed armed figures, remaining concealed behind trees or boulders. They weren't convulsing or choking to death among the drifting smoke from the fiery wreckage. It told the soldier the nerve-gas charges hadn't been set off during the initial onslaught. It was pure luck, considering all the explosions, flying bullets, that no poisonous clouds were dropping friend and foe alike. Even still, Bolan was ready to take the protective mask off his harness at a moment's notice. It was risky, either way, moving into the killzone, the enemy strangling on its desperate last gasp.

Bolan and his commandos, holding back on the triggers of their M-16s, dropped four enemy gunners who charged them from a pocket in the south foothills.

The din of weapons fire and the sharp cries of men in pain assaulted Bolan's senses. The enemy would go down to the last man. His adversaries had managed to seize a momentary advantage with their T-54s, superior numbers and the ZSU-23-4, but the soldier saw the enemy was now pinned down. They were hemmed in by Grimaldi's gunship to the north, along with the ground forces to south and from the rear by Bolan and his commandos, who had made their blind side.

In the distance he saw the Apache was forced to soar off behind the south ridgeline as the T-54 thundered away, the tank rolling out of the gorge, turret swinging, barrel tracking in a desperate attempt to nail the gunship.

Grimaldi, though, had just knocked out the ZSU-23-4. There was nothing left of the antiaircraft cannon but warped and smoking metal.

Firelight enabled Bolan to shed his NVD goggles. The stench of roasting flesh, burning oil and cordite in his nose, the Executioner raked the south foothills of the gorge with a long burst of 5.56 mm autofire. Choosing targets at will, Bolan nailed at least a half-dozen Shiites before they knew what hit them.

Then the enemy began running pell-mell from the foothills. Hit from behind and above by the American commando force, the combined Shiite and Lebanese military force had nowhere to run. Judging from the ceaseless stammer of autofire from along the south ridge, Bolan knew the bulk of the commandos had escaped the blast that had downed their gunship.

It was still far from over.

Bolan noted the discarded RPG-7 rocket launchers among the strewed bodies of the Shiites. He also saw three SAM-7 guided-missile launchers among the dead.

Suddenly the Apache banked over the south ridge and loosed a Hellfire missile. A heartbeat later the T-54 was pulverized to fiery shards of flying scrap.

Bolan triggered his M-203 as his two commandos fired their M-16s on a group of Shiites and uniformed Lebanese soldiers near the mouth of the gorge. The Executioner scored paydirt as his 40 mm grenade impacted, dead center, into a group of fanatics, the blast shredding their numbers, hurling bodies everywhere across the graveyard of flaming wreckage.

Still the enemy appeared hell-bent on a savage fighting withdrawal. Smoke and flames danced across the mouth of the gorge. For a long moment Bolan's view was obscured by the wall of smoke and fire. Peering, he saw at least three vehicles bulldoze through scattered debris, whiplash around the corner of the gorge.

Grimaldi zeroed in on the pockets of enemy survivors in the gorge, or armed Shiites running for their lives. The Huey swooped into the gorge, minigun flaming, rockets streaking away to add to the murderous mop-up.

Bolan let his friend go at it. He gave their rear and flanks a hard search. Nothing moved, except the surviving enemy forces mowed down, sent flying or spread over the floor of the gorge by Grimaldi's relentless death from above.

Towers patched through to Bolan. "I've got wounded up here. I need Griswald to get up here right away for evac."

"You've got runners, Major," Bolan answered. The soldier was moving for a Land Rover still intact. Bolan saw he was down to two 40 mm grenades for his M-203. A quick search of the dead, and he found then hauled in an armed RPG-7.

"I didn't see anything leave this gorge, Belasko."

During the chaos and confusion of battle, Bolan figured the major had missed the enemy's run.

"I did, Major. Three vehicles. Heading north. I'm going after them."

"Belasko, I want that area secured!"

Bolan hopped into the Land Rover, found the keys in the ignition and fired up the engine.

"Use the Apache and my pilot to cut off the runners," Bolan told Towers.

"Belasko, I'm giving you a direct order. Stay put!"

"You can send the Apache as air-fire support or leave me on my own. Your call," Bolan said, then severed radio contact with Towers. Calhoun, Kuschka and their remaining gunners, he believed, were escaping for the Lebanese CP. Bolan wasn't about to lose his prime targets again. As he plowed the Land Rover through a hunk of twisted metal, the soldier dialed in the frequency on his handheld to raise Grimaldi.

"Striker to Skywatcher, come in."

"Skywatcher here."

Looking in his side mirror, Bolan saw the Apache lower into the gorge, while Grimaldi kept the Huey hovering along the north ridge.

"I'm going after three vehicles that just evacuated the gorge, Skywatcher. Can you cover me?"

"I'm way down on firepower, Striker."

Bolan gritted his teeth, having feared just that answer from Grimaldi. It would be too risky for the ace pilot to cover him from the air if the enemy had any more surprises waiting. If Towers's intel was accurate about the Lebanese military compound, then two Russian attack choppers were waiting. The Huey would prove no match for the Hinds, low on firepower or not.

Bolan decided to go at it on his own.

"Help the major secure the gorge, Skywatcher. Pass the word again to Towers I'll need that Apache."

He heard Grimaldi curse but confirm the order.

BOLAN SOON FOUND he was marked for an ambush. He had been spotted by his quarry, who had most likely radioed ahead.

Fisting the Land Rover's wheel, Bolan drove hard down the dirt stretch that hugged the foothills of the mountains. The sky was brightening, and it wouldn't be long before daylight washed over the Bekaa Valley. Concealment by shadows or any form of cover going into the target was out of the question. Here and there in the distance, the soldier spotted stone huts, what appeared ancient temple ruins to the east. Other than that, it looked as if the Lebanese military unit and the terrorists had claimed this piece of the Bekaa for themselves.

Dead ahead he saw the large tents, then he saw the armed soldiers, the two T-54s and other military vehicles that signaled Bolan he was making a straight charge for the Lebanese command post.

It was the two Russian attack choppers, though, that grabbed Bolan's attention in the next instant. Moments ago he had just seen the three target vehicles barrel down the east side of the tents. Armed Lebanese soldiers, fifteen to twenty in all, were scrambling from the tents, securing the perimeter, armed with assault rifles and rocket launchers. Bolan was nearly on top of the compound.

Out of nowhere the Executioner was suddenly facing overwhelming odds. It wasn't the first time he had to face down a seemingly insurmountable force. But he was out there, alone, against two Mil Mi-24 Hinds, two T-54 tanks and at least two full squads of the enemy. If Towers really wanted to go the distance and nail the enemy, he would send in backup. Either way, Bolan was on his own right then. Before the sudden threat of the gunships, he had decided to take up position in the foothills, use what firepower he had left. If nothing else, he hoped to stage a standoff with the enemy until, he hoped, backup arrived. Towers seemed too hungry to crush the enemy to just let Bolan go at it himself.

And if the enemy was set to attempt to fly off again for the next phase of the operation, Bolan had hoped to get one shot at the aircraft with the RPG-7.

All that was before the gunships showed.

Now the Hinds soared toward his rear. Bolan threw the wheel hard to the left as the gunships opened up with machine-gun fire. The Executioner jounced the Land Rover down a ditch as the twin lines of tracking bullets blew past the passenger's side. Suddenly Bolan lost control of the vehicle as he barreled out of the ditch and ran the tires on the passenger's side over a boulder. The wheel seemed to have a life of its own as it wrenched itself from Bolan's hands.

Out of the corner of his eye, the soldier saw the gunships sweep past him as the Land Rover rolled up over the boulder, then flipped on its side. Metal rended and glass shattered as the soldier rode out the tumble, his head slamming off the roof. There had been no choice but to attempt an evasive maneuver, make a run from the gunships. Avoiding the first strafing run by driving wildly out of the line of fire had saved his life—but only for the moment.

The gunships would return.

The soldier tasted the blood in his mouth, flowing from a cut across his forehead, inflicted by flying glass. Giving his surroundings a quick check, he found the vehicle had rolled into a gully.

Bolan knew he had only seconds to act. He grabbed up his M-16 and the RPG-7. He heard the whapping bleat of the rotor blades in the distance, fading at first, then growing louder in his ears. They were coming back.

Kicking out the jagged shards of the windshield, Bolan rolled through the opening, ignoring the slivers digging into his shoulders and back, and scuttled out from under the overturned vehicle.

It would be dicey, waiting for the gunships to show for his intended counterattack. If they were flying back to check the gully without opening fire first, the soldier knew he stood a slim chance of blowing them out of the air.

Scrambling for the far side of the gully, Bolan saw the dust storm kicked up beyond his position. He would get one shot with the RPG-7, and his M-203 was already loaded with a 40 mm grenade in the breech. He unslung the M-16 and set it on the ground beside him.

The first of the two Hinds loomed overhead, maybe thirty yards beyond the lip of the gully. At that range it was a chipshot for Bolan.

The Executioner triggered the rocket launcher, and as

the warhead streaked away, he was already grabbing up the M-16. The warhead slammed into the nose of the Hind, the ensuing blast shearing off the nose of the gunship, sending the suddenly unmanned chopper into a death spiral. For a long moment Bolan was forced to hug the side of the gully as wreckage blew overhead.

The warrior never got the chance to finish off Hind number two.

Another ear-shattering blast thundered directly beyond Bolan's cover, and the ground trembled beneath him. Fire and smoke boiled over the gully with hurricane force. Through the deafening crackling of fire, feeling the terrible force of the earth shaking beneath him as the pulverized wreckage hammered the ground, Bolan scrambled up the gully.

Beyond the flaming mounds, he saw the Apache gunship. The helmeted two-man crew gave Bolan the thumbs-up. Towers had come through.

The pilot pointed straight ahead, then the Apache's nose dipped and the gunship streaked on for the command post.

Bolan was out of the gully and running hard for what he hoped was a final and fatal confrontation for his enemies. He watched as the Apache made a low and hard strafing run for the command post. The compound erupted with gunfire as the T-54s belched payloads. Weapons fire tracked the Apache, and Bolan feared the worst for the pilots who had most likely saved his life.

It turned ugly for the home team in the next few seconds.

Bolan hit a crouch, loosed a 40 mm hell-bomb from his M-203.

Hellfire missiles shot away from the wings of the Apache. It was nearly too little too late, and the harsh reality of combat hit home for the Apache. Even still, the Hellfires proved true tank killers.

A tidal wave of explosions dropped over the Lebanese troops. The T-54s were obliterated into blazing scrap. Bolan's warhead tore through a pocket of troops firing from the west edge of the tents. Bodies were launched in all directions, stick figures sailing through the tent, collapsing the front of the structure with their deadweight or the gale force of flying wreckage tearing gaping holes through the canvas.

As the inferno ripped through the compound, Bolan glimpsed at least three warheads sizzling for the Apache at near point-blank range.

Towers's flyboys never knew what hit them.

The pilots had been so intent on razing the compound, eliminating most of the enemy to pave the way for Bolan to search out and destroy the ground troops, they had no time to evade the missiles. The Apache was blown out of the sky.

On the run, searching for new targets, Bolan skirted from the fireball that seemed to hover directly beside him before slamming to the earth.

He reloaded the M-203's breech with his last 40 mm grenade. On the fly, his senses choked by smoke, burning oil and toasted flesh, he spotted the rocket team. They were scurrying from the T-54 ruins when Bolan hosed them with a long burst of autofire. Quickly he fed the M-16 with a fresh clip, then searched for more surviving gunmen.

Forging onto the killzone, he discovered he didn't have to wait long. Two figures staggered like drunken sailors from the black tendrils of smoke, dead ahead. They were lifting their weapons when Bolan dropped them on their backs with a quick burst of M-16 autofire across their chests.

At first look the compound appeared totally destroyed.

Suddenly Bolan heard the shriek of jet engines somewhere far to the east.

He already knew what was happening, and lifted the M-16, curling a finger around the trigger of the M-203. Running east, searching for the threat of wounded soldiers or possums, Bolan charged past the flaming hulls of the T-54s.

Autofire rang out, bullets stabbing through the thick smoke beside Bolan.

Feeling the slipstream of hot lead graze the back of his neck, Bolan dived to the ground, rolling up between the tank ruins. Flames licked for his face, the intense heat seeming to draw sweat from every pore in his body.

Standing, judging the direction of the autofire tracking him from his right flank, Bolan burst through the gap between the tongues of fire ahead.

M-16 swinging toward the source of the autofire, Bolan then spotted a lone Lebanese soldier, charging his way, an AK-47 tracking for the invader who had just come out of the firewall.

Then, from the corner of his eye, Bolan caught a fleeting glimpse of the sleek silver jet as it burst out of the tent. Then it was airborne. The Executioner was forced to give the Lebanese soldier his full and deadly attention, squeezing the trigger of his M-16 and dropping the soldier with a quick burst across his chest.

Wheeling, Bolan saw the jet bank sharply and soar off to the southeast. Before he knew it, the enemy was well out of range for any attempt with the M-203.

Frustration and hot anger welled in Bolan. He stood there, watching his enemies disappear in the distance. Gone, again.

Southeast. Pakistan lay in that direction.

Striding from the strewed wreckage and scattered bodies, but maintaining vigilance on his flanks and rear, Bolan felt the urgency to get in touch with Brognola and lay out the logistics, and battle strategy to pick up the hunt for the enemy.

As he cleared the smoke, Bolan heard a familiar whump-whump in the distance and spotted the Huey bearing down on the compound.

M-16 low by his side, the Executioner waited as the Huey closed. As the gunship touched down, Bolan met Grimaldi's grim stare in the cockpit. The soldier shook his head, and Grimaldi's expression turned dark. The Stony Man pilot read the anger and frustration in Bolan's gesture, knew their prime targets had escaped for Pakistan.

Then Bolan found Towers, standing tall in the doorway behind the M-60 machine gun.

"Under any other circumstances," Bolan told Towers as he noted two blacksuited commandos stretched out on the floor, hooked up to IV, their wounds attended to by a field medic, "I'd say thanks. Those Apache pilots may have saved my life."

The major nodded. The man showed no emotion. He had known the risks, going in. He had dead and wounded to get back to the base along the Israeli-Lebanon border. The man was a professional, and Bolan sensed Towers knew his job here was done. What would be left in the wake of the Lebanon commando strike was for the politicians to rail about. Of course, Bolan knew there would be a cry of outrage by the

Lebanese government for the attack on their soil by American commandos. Smoke and mirrors, Bolan knew. Beirut was a known terrorist base despite what its government might otherwise want the West to believe. And Bolan had no compulsion to grieve for the Lebanese soldiers who had fought to hide and arm the Shiite fanatics with Kuschka's shipment of nerve gas. There had been no civilian casualties, at least.

So Lebanon would boil on as a caldron for the future schemes of terrorist operations. And Bolan knew Uncle Sam would deny any knowledge of the commando strike in the Bekaa Valley.

Business as usual? So it would seem.

Right then the soldier had bigger fish to catch.

"I've got a prisoner you might like to interrogate," Towers told Bolan. "So far, on the ride in, he's told me a pretty interesting story."

Bolan looked at the sullen face seated on the bench in the cargo hold, and hopped into the gunship.

18

"I am Sergi Skaskov. I am formerly of the Soviet Union's special forces known as Spetsnaz."

"I need something more than name, rank and unit," Bolan said. "Unless you can tell me something I don't already know about Kuschka and the people he works for, we have nothing to discuss."

The Executioner sat on the bench across from the Russian. Bolan's head wound from his crash in the Land Rover had required several stitches. Other than cuts, scratches, being stiff and sore from head to toe, Bolan was ready to move on to Pakistan. With each passing moment, he knew his enemies were en route to finalize a deal that involved either component parts for a nuclear reactor, or enriched uranium and plutonium. But why go to a renegade Pakistani colonel when the Russian Mafia could have just as easily acquired the necessary components for a nuclear reactor or even stolen nuclear warheads to sell to Kuschka? It was only one of many burning questions still unanswered.

The soldier took a moment of silence to let the Russian gather himself, choose his words carefully.

Towers sat beside the prisoner, who wore a bloody bandage around his head. Apparently the Russian had been near the ZSU-23-4 when it was blown to scrap by the gunship. According to what Towers learned during his prior questioning of the prisoner, the blast had knocked the Russian off his feet and some object hammered off his skull. Towers had found him, stirring from unconsciousness, after the battle in the gorge.

Now there was a glint behind the world-weary, disillusioned look in Skaskov's eye that told Bolan the man had some intel to offer. Maybe. The soldier suspected there was a bottom-line deal for immunity in the wings, but Bolan wasn't in the position nor did he have the interest to offer the Russian a free ride at Uncle Sam's expense.

Bolan looked toward the cockpit, where Grimaldi guided the gunship over the southern Bekaa. The fuselage doors were shut, muffling the rotor noise. After the sounds of full-scale battle, it seemed amazingly quiet in the Huey.

"What's the ETA to our base, Major?"

Towers fired up a cigarette. Moments ago the medic had informed them the two blacksuits would make it, provided they received further medical treatment soon.

Towers checked his watch. "Fifteen minutes, give or take. I radioed the Israelis. They, uh, had a commando team on standby, just in case we didn't make it."

The major had neglected to tell the Stony Man warriors that item, but Bolan figured there were other details Towers had skipped, most of which detailed cleanup and evacuation and cover stories.

"They're flying in now to help secure the gorge," Towers said. "From first glance, our Shiite fanatics had enough nerve gas to wipe out half of Israel. Of course, they were in canister form, or it looks like they could be set off in an RPG-type warhead. It would have required small suicide armies to have gotten the job done."

"A lot of lives have been saved," Bolan said. "And, yeah, a lot of lives were lost."

Towers nodded, staring at Bolan with a look of new respect. "It was worth it. And for what it's worth, you'll have my full cooperation getting to Pakistan. You and Griswald showed some real balls—for special agents from the Justice Department, that is," he added, cocking a wry smile. "All bullshit aside, Belasko, you knew I wouldn't leave you hanging out to dry when you decided to take off on your own for that Lebanese CP."

"I was hopeful you wouldn't."

Major Towers smoked, nodded. "Kuschka and Calhoun and whoever their superiors are have to be stopped. They've been running wild for too long. Where this agenda of theirs will lead, who is actually involved, it's guesswork at this point."

"From what I've learned so far, their tracks have been covered by our own people inside the U.S. military and intelligence agencies. I saw a man die in Long Island who got the ball rolling and before I got involved."

"Yeah. I know all about the late ex-Senator. Whatever your involvement in what happened in New York, I don't know, don't care to know. All I know is that you want to nail these bastards and in an unofficial capacity that won't have them see their day in court. That's good enough for me. I believe in fighting fire with fire.

"When we get back to base, and you want your jet fueled, we can have you airborne as soon as we touch down. We'll get you into Pakistan. I have a contact in Karachi whose been part of a recent ongoing operation to clean up a few messes in that part of the world. I've got a jacket on this Colonel Turbat bastard for you. The CIA's been looking to nail Turbat for some time. He's got half the Pakistani army and government in his pocket. Fortunately there's still a few good people in power in that country who want the SOB's head on a stake. They've worked with the CIA, but the Pakistanis will only cooperate up to a certain point. Read the file, you'll understand why, and how Kuschka would have held hands with this Turbat all these years. Kuschka and Turbat have been instrumental in flooding Pakistan with heroin and guns, and they've been doing it for some time. The Pakistanis want to clean house. This Turbat's days appeared numbered.''

There were many things about the enemy's objectives that still weren't clear to Bolan, but he was piecing things together with each explosive leg of the mission. The opposition's ultimate goal was to engineer some form of global domination—at worst, create anarchy and revolution in targeted Third World counties, or at best, apparently step in and hold these countries hostage by chemical, biological and nuclear blackmail. So far, the enemy had been gathering money, weapons and hired men of war. To whom Kuschka and Calhoun pledged allegiance, and how their superiors in Hydra intended to pull off a reign of death and anarchy remained to be seen.

Bolan turned grim attention to the prisoner. "What have you got?"

"I have nothing to offer you," the Russian told Bolan. "However, I know where you can find the information you need, or rather a man who has the information you might need on Kuschka and his superiors. His name is Viktor Lubaska. He is a former intelligence officer in the GRU. He is a hated rival of Kuschka's. Not more than three weeks ago he and another man, Aleksandr Nikoly, a former officer in the GRU, came to my Moscow apartment. I was recruited to become part of a revolution, I was informed, about to befall Russia. Understand, after Spetsnaz, I lost everything because I could not adapt to the so-called democracy of the new Russia. There were many like us, former military, KGB, GRU. I was out of work, I drank constantly, I gambled, I stole, lied, cheated, dabbled in various criminal activities, but only to survive. My wife left me, my children abandoned me. Nikoly and Lubaska came to me, offered me a way out as they offered other selected former Spetsnaz soldiers whose lives were in a similar dead-end state.''

''And these two men were sent by Kuschka to recruit you and other former Spetsnaz troops as part of the spearhead for this new revolution,'' Bolan said.

The Russian shrugged. ''I was paid ten thousand dollars up front, in U.S. dollars, not worthless rubles. I met with Nikoly once, Lubaska twice. I was to become some reborn soldier for Kuschka's purposes, but I see now I was merely cannon fodder. It seemed Nikoly, according to Lubaska, had been whisked away to a remote Siberian outpost, an abandoned gulag. Lubaska had his own reasons for pushing my recruitment into this new army. I didn't know what to believe, but I saw a look of hate in Lubaska's eyes for Kuschka when he mentioned the man's name. Lubaska worked in the shadows, fearing, he told me, that Kuschka or another assassin would come for him anytime.

''Lubaska, it seems, is working to bring Kuschka down. There is a history between the two men, the details of which Lubaska did not tell me. There were insinuations of past wrongs. I believe Kuschka, a known and feared former KGB assassin, murdered someone close to Lubaska long ago. There was a hate and rage in his eyes that told me he regarded Kuschka as a man he needed to kill even if it meant giving up his own life first.''

''So you were to be a pawn, to get close to Kuschka and lead Lubaska to him? Get to the bottom line,'' Bolan said.

''Nikoly and Lubaska put together a file on what they knew about Kuschka's plans, who his superiors are, where they are hiding. They were intelligence officers, after all, had and still have access to certain intelligence vital to the security of Russia. But in Russia, there really are no secrets. Only corruption and schemes for power, and we are seeing this as we have never seen before. As for pertinent information you would need, Lubaska has it.''

''Where is Lubaska?'' Bolan asked.

''Moscow, last I saw him. Lubaska has long suspected a major revolution is waiting, even a revolution by nuclear blackmail, meant to overthrow this new democracy and throw Russia back to the days of Stalin.'' The Russian paused and heaved a breath. ''I am sad to say, democracy is not working in my country, but I do not think a sweeping reign of terror and anarchy will make things right.''

''I'm not a politician nor a seer,'' Bolan said. ''I want Kuschka eliminated, and I want to tear down the house of cards his superiors have built. Do you have any more to add?''

''As for who Kuschka works for, it would be with Lubaska. Lubaska has formed his own intelligence network, which works with certain individuals in the new government who fear a revolution. You work for the CIA, or whoever, and Lubaska has CIA contacts in Russia, I am sure. This is all easy enough to verify.''

Bolan looked away from the Russian and let his gaze settle on Towers. "When we land, we're gone. Can this contact of yours in Karachi help me get to Turbat?"

Towers nodded. "He's been working on a way to nail the son of a bitch for a long time. I know the man personally."

"He's black ops?"

"What else?"

"He has a team?"

"You'd have to talk to him. But if you're going after Turbat, you're going to need all the help you can get. Turbat has a small army of determined and well-trained former Pakistani soldiers. Our intelligence figures Turbat's personal army numbers somewhere around a hundred guns. Maybe more."

Bolan was already thinking ahead to some extra firepower. In fact he had already discussed it with Brognola. If the big Fed was again proving true to form in arranging logistics, then the F-15E would already be grounded, fueled and ready for combat for Grimaldi at a U.S. military base in Oman.

Bolan settled back on his bench. Right then he wasn't sure what to believe, whom to trust. But he would run with what the Russian prisoner had given him, and he knew Stony Man Farm could confirm or punch holes in the Russian's story. If a blitz into Russia was in the future, then it would have to wait. At the moment, Bolan knew Pakistan would prove another march of death that would drive both sides alike closer to oblivion. He only hoped he and Grimaldi and whoever they might link forces with in Pakistan would personally see to it their prime targets were finally annihilated.

Pakistan

THE MUSLIM VILLAGE of Sirdotaha was located in the southern province of Sind. Given the defeat they had endured and would most likely have to face again, Kuschka couldn't wait to fly on with the enriched uranium and plutonium, free himself of the stink of animal manure, sweat and pungent odors of spices and other exotic foods he had smelled when driving into the village.

With each passing minute, Kuschka felt more trapped, his nerves fraying toward some murderous outburst, while waiting for the deal to be nailed down so he and his troops, and the men he was buying from the colonel, could get airborne. Arrangements to settle their business in Pakistan, then fly on, had already been made. Only now the Russian felt an urgent need to rearrange a few details. Eventually he would have to come clean with the colonel about their recent disasters and the trouble that could follow them into Pakistan. Not now, though, he told himself, not until money changed hands and his matériel and new mercenary army was secured.

He knew personally all about Turbat's murderous temper, and he knew the Pakistani colonel wouldn't receive the news of a potential enemy assault on his home turf with merely a wink and a nod, an assurance that together they would take care of any commando strike from the shadows.

Feeling the stares of Calhoun, the Americans and what was left of his own men, Kuschka moved to the window and opened the wooden shutters. Their safehouse, he thought, and wanted to laugh bitterly, sat on a ledge, overlooking the village. Long shadows were now falling over the green fields and sparsely forested hills to the west. Below, countless villagers meandered with goats, camels, dogs among the stone huts and the open tents of the bazaar. East the green fields gave way to the sandy scrubland. Pakistan, he thought, searching inside for some moment of peace, the crossroads of Asia, where the land changed from the snowcapped peaks of the Himalayas to fertile plains to marshland to burning deserts, and almost with each province. It wasn't Kuschka's first trip to the country. He hoped it would be his last.

Since the Afghanistan war, he had made several ventures into Karachi, searching out allies who would help him smuggle heroin into the country. He had found a willing ally in Colonel Turbat. He had made the colonel a wealthy, if not hated and wanted man. The colonel owed him.

Below in the village, Kuschka spotted an AK-47, here and there, among the sea of turbans and brightly clothed women. Men toting weapons in full view of their neighbors, he knew, wasn't unusual in most parts of the world. Where life was cheap, where there were too many with too little, money and the power of the gun were worshiped. He had been to many countries, like Pakistan, where he could buy or kill his way to achieve whatever his goals.

"He'll come here. You know that, don't you?"

Kuschka wheeled, baring his teeth at Calhoun. The Americans were grouped around a wooden table, sitting in chairs or lounging against the stone walls. Kuschka fought to keep his rage choked down, resisting the urge to run across the room and shoot him in the face.

"Who is coming?"

Kuschka looked at the brown-skinned, turbaned giant standing in the far corner of the room. Moosqah had an AK-47 slung across his shoulder, but it was the hilt of the curved scimitar, tucked inside the sash around his waist, that his hand seemed to never stray too far from.

"The colonel did not get you into our country for you to bring him unnecessary trouble," Moosqah said. "If there is something I need to know, tell me now."

"We've had trouble, but it's been taken care of," Kuschka lied.

"Indeed. Is that why you are a full day late?"

"How long do we have to wait here?" Kuschka asked.

In the other rooms of the building, at least a dozen armed Pakistanis, fiercely loyal to Turbat, were smoking, lounging, waiting for the colonel's arrival. Once again the situation looked set to explode in Kuschka's face, from both his alleged allies and the threat of his American adversaries. He tried to shove out of his mind any paranoid or defeatist thoughts, but it was getting hard to remain positive in the face of near annihilation by their unknown enemies.

"I told you, the colonel is north, making certain the rest of the army you have paid for is gathered and given a final briefing. They will be flying here in the Antonov that you provided a while back."

"The colonel and I go back years," Kuschka said, glad all of a sudden he had his own AK-47 at hand. Despite the fact that his force was armed, he knew they were low on ammunition. "I can't believe he wouldn't be here."

Moosqah showed an odd smile. "To do what? Greet you with open arms? Understand, bribes had to be paid, the Pakistani military kept out of this area, which meant personal visits to officers in the Sind province."

"I understand that. I just hope he's delivering what I want."

Moosqah nodded at the duffel bags and satchels in the corner of the room. "As you delivered, so will he."

"We need weapons."

Moosqah peered at Kuschka. "So, you are expecting trouble?"

Silently Kuschka cursed Calhoun. "We have had trouble, yes, and I just want to be prepared."

"What sort of trouble?" Moosqah asked, an edge in his voice.

"Try and trust me on this. I'm working with you people, not against you."

But Kuschka was already thinking beyond the point when he would finally meet with Turbat. Getting safely out of Pakistan was the problem. A plan was forming in his mind to see them to their next destination, which only he knew. So far, the Americans had been able to find them wherever they went. Kuschka had radar-jamming equipment that was the latest in high-tech, invented by his own people in the remote base in the Russian Far East. It was capable of deflecting even signals to U.S. AWACS. But why were they still being hounded, thrashed wherever they went? Who was the enemy?

During the long flight from Lebanon, Kuschka had time to seethe over yet another near miss in the face of death. He had also lost two more men. Perhaps that had been the reason they were being followed, and attacked, almost as soon as they landed. Those missing in action from the previous engagements were still alive and talking to the Americans. He had been giving briefings to the troops all along, and he now realized he'd made a grave error in judgment. It made sense that the opposition was taking hostages, making them talk. If that wasn't the case, he intended to soon find out. Once they were clear of Pakistan, he would give Calhoun a thorough interrogation and discover if the former Special Forces major was really an ally.

Moosqah squared his shoulders, glaring at Kuschka. "The colonel has gone to great trouble to make sure he leaves this country safely with you. He feels the tightening of the noose from our people. Several of his allies in the government and the military have been found out to have been accepting his money for some time. He knows he must leave Pakistan. He is believing in you to relocate him, and those of us loyal to him, for future monetary rewards. Even if we gain temporary sanctuary in Russia, it would be better than facing certain execution in Pakistan for dealing heroin."

"Then let's get on the same page here. We need weapons, and I know you have them."

"You seem most eager to make sure you are sufficiently armed." Moosqah paused, then nodded. "Very well, I will do as you ask. However, I assure you, if you have brought some trouble to the colonel, I will not hesitate to kill you personally."

Kuschka felt his blood race with anger as the big Pakistani made a show of drumming his fingers on the hilt of his sword.

Kuschka clenched his jaw, his mouth dry with fear. Suddenly the future looked darker than ever.

19

Bolan was out of the copilot's seat of the F-15E and on the ground as soon as Grimaldi brought the fighter jet to a halt. The Executioner, having taken his gear and weapons of war from a special compartment on the fighter jet's fuselage, watched as the team of M-16-toting blacksuits filed out of the abandoned fort.

He gave his surroundings a hard surveillance. The makeshift airstrip, lined with flares, was situated on a remote plain in the Sind province of Pakistan. According to Stony Man intel, the nearest village was thirty miles north. It was the village, according to Towers's file on Turbat, where the enemy was holed up, somewhere beyond the distant north hills. The renegade colonel called the village of Sirdotaha his command post, with another, smaller village to the north where he apparently housed the bulk of his troops and contraband.

Bolan and Grimaldi were in Pakistan illegally, but they wouldn't be in the country any longer than it took to search out and destroy their enemies.

Dressed in a blacksuit, Bolan put on his webbing and harness. His Beretta 93-R was already snug in its shoulder leather, and a .44 Magnum Desert Eagle was holstered on his right hip. He slung the M-16 with attached M-203 grenade launcher across his shoulder. A small satchel bulged with grenades he would attach to his harness later.

Bolan held his ground by the runway, waiting as a stocky, crew-cut man in a blacksuit, armed with an M-16 and holstered .45 Colt, rolled up out of the deep shadows, then studied Bolan for a long moment. The silence lingered, and he wondered just what kind of reception the Stony Man warriors would receive. Bolan listened to the roar of the F-15E's engines as the fighter jet rolled to the end of the runway and turned. Grimaldi's orders were to fly south, stay in the air until the target was confirmed and isolated, then attack and annihilate enemy. Afterward Grimaldi would return to the command post and pick up Bolan.

Provided, of course, the numbers fell the way Bolan intended.

"Belasko, I have to assume?"

"Yeah."

"I'm Karball. My superiors radioed and informed me to expect you." He looked at the fighter jet as it rolled back for takeoff. "Looks like your pilot got our coordinates without a problem. I must say I didn't expect an F-15 to lend a little assistance, but given the task I'm facing, I could use all the help I can get. Whoever you people really are, you must be mighty important to be given joint command of this operation. I've spoken with Towers. He says to put you two on board, and I've never known the man to be a bad judge of character."

"You want to get me up to speed then."

Karball grunted. "Inside. Time's running out. My informant in the village just told me the colonel's landed, and we've got a fix on Calhoun and Kuschka. They made it here."

Bolan had expected nothing less since Lebanon.

"THE SHIP with our targets' merchandise left Karachi two hours ago."

Bolan lifted an eyebrow. "All of a sudden, after years of Calhoun and Kuschka operating at will, the CIA has suddenly picked up the scent? And you've known about this deal, and the one in Lebanon for how long?"

"I'm not sure I like where you may be headed with that."

"It's an honest question. I just want to know we're after the same thing. The CIA's known about Calhoun and Kuschka for a long time—that much I know. All of a sudden, wherever I look, another black-ops team is hunting for these two. It tells me I'm fumbling around in the dark, wondering who's who and what's what."

Karball shifted in his wooden chair. Powered by a generator, soft white light bathed the large room, the ghostly sheen of it washing over Karball's scowl, making the man appear menacing as anger sparked his blue eyes. The operative peered at Bolan across the table, which was littered with black-and-white pictures of their targets and maps of the targeted village and surrounding area.

"I'm sure you raised some of the same questions to Towers," Karball said. "I'm sure he told you the same thing I'm about to. I'm not here to justify my or the Company's position, their intel, lack of intel, the how and why the bad guys have been running guns, drugs, selling top-secret information to the Russians and whatever else they've been doing. I'm here, you're here. Our bad guys are sitting in the village as we speak. The opposition is slick, savvy and ballsy. It would seem they have more money than God, more contacts in key places in every critical institution in whatever country they show up in than even the CIA. They are fast becoming a global scourge and right now they are desperate to nail down a deal that would land them, eventually, nuclear firepower. My orders are clear and simple.''

Bolan mentally ran back what Karball had told him so far. The hard guess was that the combined enemy force, including Turbat's renegade army, numbered somewhere around a hundred guns. Bolan counted twenty blacksuits in the room, the operatives now cleaning their weapons, applying black greasepaint to their faces and hands. He figured at least a few more blacksuits were posted as sentries around the fort.

Bolan saw the room was a stockpile of M-16s with attached M-203 grenade launchers, LAW rocket launchers, Uzis, crates with spare clips and grenades. With a lot of help from the F-15E, Bolan figured they were facing a fifty-fifty chance of pulling off the assault. The problem was getting into the village, isolating the enemy from innocent peasants. Bolan couldn't help but again recall how the enemy would casually use human shields to hide behind while fighting back or as an escape valve.

''If nothing else, we can use your fighter jet to knock out their aircraft,'' Karball said, ''now that we know the enriched uranium and plutonium isn't with our targets. Some serious strings had to be jerked to get the Pakistanis to give us the nod on this. Last thing I want is for the Sind province to become a polluted nuclear wasteland. The Pakistanis are cooperating but only, I believe, to get some egg off their faces since a known terrorist who recently murdered U.S. citizens in our backyard claimed refuge here before he was captured.''

''Where did the uranium and plutonium come from?'' Bolan asked.

"From North Korea."

That surprised Bolan, but he didn't have time to spare on too many questions. "Why wouldn't Kuschka go to the Russian Mafia or use his connections in the military to secure a warhead in his own backyard?"

"Maybe he has. I don't know how the man thinks. Maybe the price was right for Turbat when he bought the stuff from the North Koreans because it was too risky or too costly for him to buy or steal fissionable nuclear material in Pakistan, so he's turning around and selling it for a little bigger chunk of change to Kuschka. All I know is that when this operation is over, the U.S. military will board and seize the vessel. My orders are clear. Terminate Calhoun, Kuschka and Turbat with extreme prejudice. Are you on board for that kind of action?"

"I wouldn't have it any other way."

"All right. The vehicles we'll use are out back. I see your radio and throat mike, so I'm assuming you can call your pilot in for air support."

Bolan nodded. "Let's roll. Anything else I need to know, you can fill me in on the way."

"I AM FURIOUS that you went ahead, Colonel, without orders, without informing me and sent my merchandise on a Pakistani freighter, when I thought we had an understanding it was to be flown out of this country!"

Calhoun stood with his men near the domed mosque. He listened to the angry exchange between Kuschka and the lean, dark-haired Colonel Turbat. As things felt like they were heating up and heading toward some explosion of violence, Calhoun experienced a moment's relief he was armed with an AK-47, as were the rest of his men and Kuschka's Spetsnaz commandos. A few

RPG-7s had been graciously handed out back at the hut in Sirdotaha, wielded by three of his own men. It wasn't enough if gunplay erupted, and he silently cursed. They were looking at maybe eighty of Turbat's soldiers, all of them armed with AKs or RPG-7 launchers, and now the deal looked set to fall through. Kuschka was clearly on edge, his tall silhouette framed in the glow from the flares that lined the dirt runway beside the Russian. Calhoun glanced at the grounded Antonov AN-22, its turboprop engines silent. Visions of instant and fiery destruction from the sky flamed through his mind. The transport plane and the men were ripe, sitting targets.

Something was going to go wrong. Just like before the fiasco back in the gorge of the Bekaa Valley hit them, Calhoun counted plenty of guns, Jeeps and Land Rovers. Again it was too quiet out there in the darkness of the plain. Calhoun began to fear, more than ever, that Pakistan would be the country they wouldn't leave alive.

With his men surrounding him, Calhoun checked the dark skies. Maybe thirty minutes ago Turbat had radioed Moosqah to inform him he had landed. The village where the alleged deal would go down was dark and appeared uninhabited except for all the gunmen. Most of Turbat's force waited by vehicles inside the stone wall that ringed the mosque. It felt more wrong with each passing tense second, and Calhoun couldn't keep the images of their total destruction out of his mind. Worse still, Turbat would get his money, so what would keep the Pakistanis from simply gunning them down?

"It was unavoidable," Turbat explained. "I am told by my own paid intelligence agents that the CIA is prepared to launch an attack against me and my men. Many of my own paid officials in the government and the

military have been arrested. I am cut off from further
information and assistance out of Karachi as of this
morning when several key politicians I owned were
likewise arrested. As for our deal, I began to fear you
would be further delayed. Since time was critical, I had
to make certain my men had paid the necessary bribes
in Karachi to make sure the merchandise was loaded
and the ship set sail. It was time-consuming and it cost
me a lot of money.''

''Where is that ship sailing to?''

''The Philippines, of course, where it was agreed you
would fly myself and my men.''

''You've taken a lot for granted.''

''We have done business many times in the past. Our
trafficking in heroin has made me a rich man. Right
now I have become a criminal in my own country, but
for some time I knew I would have to flee Pakistan. I
cannot afford to take anything for granted.''

''Need I remind you you used my contacts, my routes
from Afghanistan, my planes, my mules, at least in the
beginning, to make you rich?''

''Indeed, I owe you much.''

Kuschka shot a murderous glare around at the armed
Pakistanis. ''Here's what we do. I fly on now. I will be
in contact with you once we are airborne. I want you
to give me the frequency by which I can raise the captain of this ship.''

''And my money?''

Calhoun listened as Kuschka barked an order over
his shoulder in Russian. A Spetsnaz soldier moved away
from one of the Land Rovers that had transported them
from Sirdotaha. He dropped the satchel at the feet of
the Pakistani colonel.

''That is half of the agreed-upon price.''

Turbat scowled. "What? This is unacceptable."

"You did not let me finish. Once we're in the air, once I have raised the captain of this vessel, I will give you further instructions on our course. I have plenty of contacts in the Far East, but there is another landing site I have in mind from which I can board this vessel and take my merchandise. I will decide the ship's final destination later."

"You do not trust me?"

"Further, to make certain we do not lose each other's trust, I will order three of my own soldiers, and three of the American major's soldiers, to fly with you. You give me four of your best men to fly with us. That way, we can all keep an eye on each other. Agreed?"

Turbat's anger faded. The Pakistani colonel realized he had overstepped his bounds by acting on his own.

Turbat nodded. "Very well, but we will be in radio contact by the hour."

"I would not have it any other way, Colonel."

Calhoun searched the skies again. Then he heard Turbat snarl, "Why does he keep looking at the sky like that? It is making me extremely nervous."

"Major, pick three men, then board the jet. We're out of here."

Calhoun searched the faces of his surviving force. Three men, he thought, and again felt that same sinking feeling he'd experienced before, instinct warning him that he was about to lose yet more men. The way it was all shaping up, Calhoun began to think he might be alone, and real soon.

BOLAN AND KARBALL led half of the commando team up the rise. They were going for a flanking maneuver, with the other half of the commando force moving up

the north slope of the hill. Once they reached the wall
ringing the large stone structure, they would go over the
wall, run the short stretch of no-man's-land to the building, go in hard through the south and back doorways.
Karball said that if it was armed and moving, shoot it.

Bolan maintained grim focus on the stone hut above
as he cradled his M-16. The target house overlooked
the large village. It was a perfect vantage point for the
enemy to watch the far-reaching plain in both directions
and the village below.

At that time of night, other than a few roving Pakistanis near the bazaars and a light on, here and there,
in the tiered homes, Bolan found very little activity in
Sirdotaha. Karball had briefed Bolan there were no reg-
ular Pakistani military patrols or outposts within fifty
miles, which meant next to nothing to Bolan. The jacket
on Turbat made the colonel out to be one of the most
ruthless and powerful drug lords in Middle Asia. That
he had been operating at large in Pakistan for so long
meant plenty of drug money had been spread around to
buy him this safe haven.

Bolan looked at the light spilling from the window
of the south face of the target building. A shadow
spread over the window, then a turbaned silhouette, toting an AK-47, appeared in the window a moment later.
The gunman in the window gave the courtyard a quick
look. Bolan and the other commandos hit the ground in
prone positions. They were just below the rise, and the
lookout shouldn't have spotted them.

With each passing moment, Bolan felt an urgent need
to get to the second village. Instinct warned him his
prime targets weren't in Sirdotaha. But Karball had insisted on hitting the secondary target first, claiming they
needed to eliminate any threat to their rear if reinforce-

ments were called up from the village. Considering the enemy numbers, Bolan had little choice right then but to ride with Karball's program.

Bolan peeked over the rise, saw the sentry vanish from the window. Karball patched through to the leader of the second unit, said in a near whisper, "We're right on top of them. Start counting off now. Thirty seconds."

As a group they charged the wall. On the run, Bolan vaulted the three-foot wall with Olympic grace, landed, searching for the sudden show of enemy targets. As previously planned, Bolan and Karball would go through the door first, the Executioner low, the CIA operative high.

They were running across the short stretch of no-man's-land when the sentry showed in the window. Bolan made brief eye contact with the hardman. The Pakistani was about to shout a warning when a short burst from Bolan's M-16 drilled him in the chest, punching him back, out of sight.

But they had lost the edge of surprise. Shouting erupted from inside the stone hut.

"I'll kick in the door. Frag 'em," Karball growled.

Bolan and Karball flanked the doorway, the Executioner arming a frag grenade. The operative caved in the door with a thundering kick. Autofire cut loose from beyond the doorway, and the chatter of weapons fire erupted from somewhere deeper in the building.

Unit two had made it in.

Bolan hurled the steel egg through the door as bullets chewed up wood and stone above his head. The grenade blew, generating shrill cries of pain as countless lethal bits of shrapnel razored through the enemy beyond.

The two men charged through the doorway, into the

cordite and the swirling smoke. Several armed figures raced toward them through a beaded archway. They were momentarily frozen by the sight of still more black-garbed commandos swarming into the hut.

Holding back on the trigger of his M-16, Bolan joined Karball in mowing down the trio beyond the pall of smoke.

When they dropped, stitched to crimson ruins, Bolan was surging ahead, spotting a man reaching for a mike at a radio console. Bolan cut loose with his assault rifle, drilling the guy with an extended burst up his spine that slammed him into the radio console. Sparks and blood flew around the spinning figure before he collapsed to the floor.

Unit two poured into the room. "We're clear," the pointman told Karball.

"How many?" Karball asked.

"Six targets neutralized, sir."

"Shit. What, ten bad guys in all?"

"We need to get to the primary target, Karball. If you were looking to shave the numbers, this was hardly scratching the surface."

Karball told his men, "Let's pull out."

He turned to Bolan. "How soon can you get that fighter jet here?"

"He's circling the prime target now," Bolan said. "About twenty klicks east of the target site."

"Radio him and tell him to move in but wait for my order to hit them with everything he's got."

20

Several aspects of the assault against the renegade Pakistani colonel disturbed Bolan. First, how did Karball plan to tackle a hundred guns with twenty men, unless he had major backup, either in the form of legitimate Pakistani troops or a few F-16s or Mirage fighter jets used by the Pakistani military? Or was Karball acting on his own, another covert Company operation meant to terminate Turbat, even seize his heroin or cash on hand, to be diverted into CIA slush funds? It wouldn't be the first time, Bolan knew, that a renegade faction in the CIA was acting on its own for personal gain. After all, the uncovering of rogue elements in the American intelligence and military communities was how Bolan's intercontinental manhunt had been launched.

Last, but far from least, Bolan strongly suspected he wouldn't find Kuschka and Calhoun at the primary target site. It was nothing he could put his finger on; it was simply dark and nagging instinct telling him that the two men had flown on, and Bolan didn't have a clue where he could track them down next. After all, with the fissionable nuclear matériel already out to sea, why would Kuschka and Calhoun hang around in Pakistan and risk another full-scale assault.

It was too late now, Bolan saw.

The soon-to-be besieged and supposedly civilian-free

village was less than two hundred yards ahead. Already the ten-vehicle convoy of armor-plated military-style jeeps, each vehicle with an M-60 gunner in the rear, was peeling off in a classic pincer attack on the compound as it cleared the shallow rise.

And the thunder of the F-15E was already rolling in from the west. From that direction, the Executioner found the dark but unmistakable shape of the fighter jet, less than three miles out, he figured, and closing fast, low and hard.

Everything was timing for this assault, and so far, Bolan believed it would fall by the numbers.

The soldier rode on the passenger's side of the jeep, his M-16/M-203 combo ready, his webbing and harness loaded with grenades.

Karball's gruff voice shot over the radio frequency that tied in the whole commando unit. "All drivers, kill your lights! Rocket teams, disperse now and fire at will!"

Even as his driver killed the lights, Bolan could clearly take in the compound, which was lit by flares, enemy vehicle lights and lanterns near the mosque. Giant fuel trucks were unhooking hoses from the Antonov transport plane. The area around the domed mosque was a beehive of enemy activity. Suddenly, though, the countless gunmen around the transport plane, near the scattered vehicles inside the wall that ringed the dome or standing near the front entrance of the mosque froze at the sound of the fighter jet. Then gunfire erupted from behind the wall as Bolan saw shadowy figures pointing at the line of dispersing jeeps.

Bolan patched through to Grimaldi as the F-15E swooped low for the target site. "Striker to Skywatcher, come in."

"Skywatcher here, Striker."

"Fire at will."

Grimaldi did.

So did the rocket teams that had jumped from pre-designated jeeps that sluiced to sudden halts, dispersing the blacksuits with LAWs.

A fireball flashed out of the corner of the Executioner's eye. He saw one jeep hurled skyward, then spotted the RPG rocket teams scrambling just inside the walls.

"Get me to the far west side of the mosque. Go around the plane wreckage!" Bolan told his driver as lead thudded off the sides and front of the jeep.

Bolan watched for several long moments as the jet unloaded its payload on the compound. It was a fearsome sight, as two Sidewinders flamed away from the wings of the fighter jet. At point-blank range the transport plane was vaporized by a fireball that mushroomed to mountainous dimensions, the roar of the blast splitting the night asunder. A Sparrow missile then added yet more fiery horror to the inferno. Antonov wreckage was scything through runners, hurling stick figures in all directions. With any luck, judging from the devastation that dropped over them and shredded their numbers, Bolan hoped half the enemy numbers were shaved during the initial onslaught.

Return enemy fire abruptly stopped as the rocket teams pounded the ranks of Turbat's rogue army. Screams of terror and pain knifed the air as Bolan's driver raced the jeep to the far side of what was left of the Antonov. To his far left flank, Bolan saw enemy vehicles were uprooted, crushed or blown to flaming obliteration as Grimaldi soared over the compound, strafing runners and vehicles with an extended burst of

M-61 Vulcan cannon fire. Thundering lines of HE blasts further shredded the enemy ranks during the combined lightning air and ground attack.

As the jeep raced past the fiery bed of wreckage and delayed explosions rocked the night, Bolan ordered the driver to stop.

Over his shoulder, the soldier told their M-60 gunner, "Cover me! Pour it on! Follow me in, stay on my rear!"

The Executioner hopped out of the jeep. Intense firelight wavered over the compound. Bolan had a clear view in all directions around the killing field, and was searching for anything armed and coming on.

In the distance Grimaldi went into a roll. The F-15E was coming back for another killing strafe. Bolan needed to reach Grimaldi, lay out his position and the positions of the CIA operatives, separate the bad guys from the home team.

Right away Bolan picked targets, chopping down a trio of gunmen who ran his way, the soldier kicking the enemy off their feet with a long burst of M-16 autofire. Nearby human torches flailed and shrieked around the pulped ruins of jeeps and Land Rovers. The Executioner spared a few mercy rounds from his M-16.

Suddenly something strange happened to add even more horror and chaos to the battle. The firestorm from the initial strike seemed to gather a life of its own as it belched out shrieking tongues of fire and dropped a wall of flames over scattered vehicles that were still in one piece. Bolan felt the fury of the inferno nearby, felt a wind, but it was like some vortex swirling out from near the flaming sea of the Antonov, sucking in debris, and men. Several delayed explosions then thundered across the courtyard as gas tanks ignited. It was as if the fire had come to life around him. Bolan felt a sucking heated wind reaching out for him, so strong it began to lift him off his feet as if the firestorm were a vacuum.

The Executioner dived behind an intact jeep, grabbed its bumper as the fires meshed into a howling blaze, sucking gunmen across the courtyard, dragging them, kicking and screaming, into its hungry maw. The series of explosions and the roar of fire became deafening. A tidal wave of wreckage razored over Bolan's head, slamming into his cover. A shrieking wail of men in horrible agony rent the air, then faded suddenly as the firestorm seemed to fold in on itself.

Bolan put the frightening image out of his mind, though it was something that momentarily struck him as what could have happened during the firebombing of Tokyo, or German cities during World War II. He stood and raised Grimaldi as the jet began its deadly run for the hellzone.

"I'm on the west edge!" he told the Stony Man pilot. "By the mosque and on the east side of the wall, you've got large bodies of targets! Home team has secured the west end of the wall. Copy that!"

"That's affirmative, Striker!"

Another Sparrow missile then a Sidewinder streaked from the jet, slamming into the mosque where at least thirty gunmen were attempting to seek cover. They were blown clear across the compound among the flying debris and the screaming fire.

Bolan wheeled as a group of shadows poured through a wall of smoke on his flank. They were screaming in their native tongue, and began to fire AK-47s when Bolan's rear cover unloaded with the M-60, mowing them down with heavy 7.62 mm NATO lead. The jeep streaked past the soldier as he zigzagged toward the

piles of rubble in front of the mosque. Maybe ten gunmen were sliding over slabs of debris, firing their AK-
47s with long wild bursts at the jeeps and blacksuits
streaming across the large courtyard.

Bolan triggered his M-203, driving a fireball into the
nest of gunmen near the mosque. The enemy raced
across the battlefield in all directions. Gunners staggered, cried in pain or made all-out runs from the smoking rubble of the front wall. Many enemy soldiers held
their ground and died where they stood. The bark of
autofire and machine-gun fire, the roar of the infernos
near him, was a relentless and near deafening assault
on Bolan's senses.

And his feeling that his prime targets weren't within
killing reach kept growing, nagging him, but urging him
to discover if his hunch was right.

Suddenly a giant bald man raced from a wall of black
smoke, screaming at the top of his lungs. In the wavering firelight Bolan clearly recognized one of Calhoun's
thugs. The giant was covered in blood, his AK-47 flaming wild rounds in Bolan's direction. The Executioner
dived behind a pile of rubble near the mosque as lead
stitched the ground behind him. He came up, saw the
giant hurl the empty AK-47 away and grab for a side
arm. Bolan hosed him down with a quick burst of 5.56
mm lead across the chest.

He bounded over the rubble, closing on the bald giant, checking his rear and flanks. He cut loose on a trio
of runners dead ahead, flinging them to the blood-
soaked earth. Sporadic explosions sounded as Bolan
saw blacksuits, darting from wreckage, around walls of
fire, hurling grenades at any group of renegade Pakistani
soldiers engaging them in a fighting withdrawal.

Eyes peeled, Bolan loomed over the dying giant.

"You..."

"It's me. Where's Calhoun?"

The giant cursed. "Gone...long gone..."

The giant laughed, then died.

Scanning the battlefield, Bolan once again felt an overwhelming sense of frustration. He looked west, made out the shape of the F-15E. Even before he patched through to Grimaldi, Bolan suspected what he would hear from the Stony Man pilot. The enemy had flown, quick and fast in their speedy jet, out of radar range even for the sophisticated and latest in high-tech instruments aboard the fighter jet. Or Grimaldi had picked up other air traffic in the vicinity but opted to steer clear in case a few Pakistani F-16s were in the area.

The Executioner stood among the dead, the dying, and those few enemy soldiers left standing who were now throwing down their weapons and raising their arms.

No matter what it took, Bolan would pick up the trail and hunt down his enemies. There was no place on earth where they could run far enough, hide deep enough.

They had escaped him this night. Tomorrow would prove something else altogether.

CALHOUN WAS PREPARED for the worst possible news. He was sitting with his men in the rear of the jet. On each side of the cabin, just ahead, the four Pakistanis sat opposite each other, including the huge Moosqah, whose hand never strayed far from the hilt of his fearsome sword.

Calhoun stared out the porthole at the darkness beyond the jet. His AK-47 was canted against the seat beside him. The longer Kuschka remained in the cockpit with his pilots, on the radio, Calhoun suspected, the more the ex–Special Forces major grew worried.

He figured they had been flying south for ninety minutes. He saw nothing below but blackness beyond the jet for as far as he could see, not even the lights of a passing freighter. He presumed they were flying over the Arabian Sea.

He had left behind his three best men, Augustly, Bittertown and Drexsall. Bitterly he recalled how a cruelly grinning Kuschka, barking for Calhoun to pick volunteers, had then pointed at his own men and ordered them to stay behind.

It was all falling apart.

Calhoun was braced for a gun battle at twenty thousand feet, which would be suicide. One bullet hole in a window, and the whole jet would come apart.

Suddenly the cockpit door opened. For a long moment Calhoun found himself stared down by Kuschka. The Makarov pistol looked three times its size in Calhoun's fear-gripped gaze, hanging just below the Russian's shoulder. Something was terribly wrong. The silence was deafening.

Calhoun watched, waited, as Kuschka went to one of his soldiers and whispered something in his ear. The Pakistanis, Calhoun saw, tensed on the edge of their seats.

The man Kuschka had spoken to moved and said something in a low voice to the other Spetsnaz commandos in his own tongue. After all these years of dealing with the KGB, Calhoun wished he had learned more than a few Russian phrases or curse words. His heart pounding in his ears, he watched as Kuschka walked toward the Pakistanis.

"Comrades, listen up," Kuschka said. "I have some bad news and I have some very bad news."

Without warning, the Russians all stood and aimed their AK-47s at Calhoun and his people.

"What the hell is going on, Kuschka?" Calhoun rasped, but his angry voice sounded weak in his ears, coming from a great distance.

Moosqah, his expression twisted with fear and indignation, began to rise. Suddenly Kuschka drew his Makarov and shot two Pakistanis in the face. Blood flew into Calhoun's eyes, momentarily blinding him. Through the stinging haze, Calhoun saw another Russian shoot a third Pakistani in the head at point-blank range. Moosqah leaped to his feet, drawing his sword, but Kuschka's Makarov barked twice, the bullets drilling into the knees of the Pakistani, who toppled to the floor. Viciously Moosqah began to curse the Russian.

Calhoun froze in his seat as he found himself staring down the Russian guns.

"I just radioed your vessel," Kuschka snarled at Moosqah, who was clutching his shattered knees, his face a mask of hate and agony. "Do you know who answered? An American colonel who says the vessel is now the property of the U.S. military and for me to identify myself or be tracked by radar and blown out of the sky. It would appear Turbat's overzealousness, fear, paranoia, whatever, has cost me my merchandise."

Calhoun swallowed hard as Kuschka bent to put the muzzle of the Makarov against Moosqah's forehead. "Since I have not heard from or been able to raise your Colonel Turbat, I must assume he has either been arrested or killed by an enemy who has been hounding me for days and will continue to hunt me like some wild animal until I am dead. My whole operation—

indeed, my entire life—is now threatened. Our deal, Comrade Moosqah, is now null and void.''

The Makarov cracked in Kuschka's hand, and Moosqah's head snapped back, blood and bone fragments spraying from the back of his skull.

Kuschka rose, and Calhoun found himself the furious focus of the Russian's stare. The major clenched his jaw, felt his hand shaking with fear, inching toward the AK-47. Out of the corner of his eye, he found his men tensed and poised to grab up their assault rifles.

''Now, Major,'' the scar-faced Russian said, lifting the Makarov, ''you see how angry, how serious I am. How I deal with those who betray me or cause me grief. Let's hope the rest of our journey is uneventful.''

Don't miss the exciting conclusion of
THE HYDRA TRILOGY.
Look for The Executioner #243,
ASSAULT REFLEX,
in March.

Venture Deeper into the Deathlands Odyssey...

JAMES AXLER

DEATH LANDS®

ENCOUNTER

An all-new COLLECTOR'S EDITION Deathlands title!

Go back to the beginning with original editorial material, and discover the special collector's information located at the back of this longer-length novel!

Stories of the Trader and his convoy of war wagons endure in the badlands of post-holocaust America. A dealer in Deathlands' most precious commodities—weapons and fuel—Trader takes note of a young Ryan Cawdor. Surrounded in myth and rumor, Trader sets into motion the beginnings of a legend at a place called Virtue Lake....

Don't miss your chance to catch this unique collector's edition!

Available in February 1999
at your favorite retail outlet.

GOLD EAGLE®

James Axler

OUTLANDERS™

HELLBOUND FURY

Kane and his companions find themselves catapulted into an alternate reality, a parallel universe where the course of events in history is dramatically different. What hasn't changed, however, is the tyranny wrought by the Archons on mankind…this time, with human "allies."

Book #1 in the new Lost Earth saga, a trilogy that chronicles our heroes' paths through three very different alternate realities…where the struggle against the evil Archons goes on….

THE LOST EARTH SAGA
BOOK 1

Shadow THE EXECUTIONER®
as he battles evil for 352 pages of heart-stopping action!

SuperBolan®

#61452	DAY OF THE VULTURE	$5.50 U.S.	☐
		$6.50 CAN.	☐
#61453	FLAMES OF WRATH	$5.50 U.S.	☐
		$6.50 CAN.	☐
#61454	HIGH AGGRESSION	$5.50 U.S.	☐
		$6.50 CAN.	☐
#61455	CODE OF BUSHIDO	$5.50 U.S.	☐
		$6.50 CAN.	☐
#61456	TERROR SPIN	$5.50 U.S.	☐
		$6.50 CAN.	☐

(limited quantities available on certain titles)

TOTAL AMOUNT	$
POSTAGE & HANDLING	$
($1.00 for one book, 50¢ for each additional)	
APPLICABLE TAXES*	$ _____
TOTAL PAYABLE	$ _____
(check or money order—please do not send cash)	

To order, complete this form and send it, along with a check or money order for the total above, payable to Gold Eagle Books, to: **In the U.S.:** 3010 Walden Avenue, P.O. Box 9077, Buffalo, NY 14269-9077; **In Canada:** P.O. Box 636, Fort Erie, Ontario, L2A 5X3.

Name: _____

Address: _____ City: _____

State/Prov.: _____ Zip/Postal Code: _____

*New York residents remit applicable sales taxes.
Canadian residents remit applicable GST and provincial taxes.

GSBBACK1